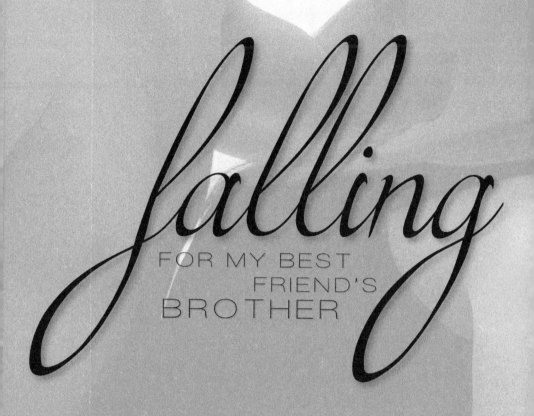

falling

FOR MY BEST
FRIEND'S
BROTHER

D1279814

new york times bestselling authors
J. S. COOPER
& HELEN COOPER

OTHER BOOKS BY J.S. COOPER

falling

FOR MY BEST FRIEND'S BROTHER

Cover design by Louisa Maggio of LM Creations.

Editing by Lorelei Logsdon.

Formatting by Inkstain Interior Book Designing.

To all the women who have loved someone from afar.

He might just feel the same way you do!

ACKNOWLEDGMENTS

To my beta readers Kathy Shreve, Cathy Reale, Cilicia White, Tanya Skaggs, Rebecca Kenmore, Kanae Eddings, Barbara Goodwin, Stacy Hahn, Katrina Jaekley, Elizabeth Rodriguez, Trisha, Emily Kirkpatrick, Kerri Long, Tianna Croy, and Gwen Midgyett, thank you for all of your feedback reading chapters of this book. I so appreciated the help perfecting certain scenes.

To all of my readers, both old and new, thank you for taking a chance on one of my books.

To God, thank you for all of your blessings.

PROLOGUE

I keep on falling

I HAVE A PIECE OF advice for you. Never fall in love with your best friend's brother. Don't fall for his boyish smile or his gorgeous big blue eyes. Don't fall for his bulging biceps or his arrogant smirk. There's nothing good that can come from falling for him. Trust me, I know. My name's Alice, and I have the biggest crush on my best friend Liv's brother, Aiden. He's everything I want in a man, aside from the fact that he's brooding, over-protective, annoying, and too devastatingly handsome for his own good.

Aiden Taylor is everything I wanted in a man, but he is the one man that I can't have. He's the one man I can't let myself be with. I couldn't afford to date him and then have everything go wrong. Liv is my best friend and like my sister, and if I dated Aiden and it didn't work out, I'd be scared that it would ruin our relationship as well. Plus, I'm scared about what would happen if the truth came out. You see, there are secrets about Aiden and me that nobody knows about. Secrets that neither of us wants found out.

However, sometimes a secret has to come out. Sometimes it's not the secret that's the issue. Sometimes the issue is you.

ONE

Never take your own advice

"ALICE, YOU NEED TO LEARN to take your own advice." Liv wriggled her eyebrows at me as she changed the channel on the TV. Her brown doe-like eyes gazed at me with a challenge, and I stifled a groan. I knew that look well. As well I should, as I was the one who had taught it to her.

"What advice is that?" I said as I casually picked up the bowl of popcorn from the coffee table and sat back. I took a couple of kernels and popped them into my mouth, enjoying the buttery sweetness as I waited for her to say the words I was dreading to hear.

"You need to have a one-night stand with Aiden." She grinned at me and I groaned. "Don't groan at me, Alice." She grabbed some popcorn and sat back on the new tan leather couch we'd recently bought.

"Careful how you're eating," I said in a proper voice. "We don't want butter on the new couch." I laughed as she made a face at me. "Also, I'm not going to have a one-night stand with your brother." I looked at the TV screen as my heart raced. I'm not going to lie, I've thought about sleeping (and when I say sleeping, I mean anything but sleeping) with Aiden for years. But he's never seen me as anything more than his little sister's best friend. And even then I don't think he really paid much attention to me. Well, technically that's not really true. There was one night that he saw me as more than 'silly little Alice.' There was one night that he saw me as a woman, but I'm not going to talk about that.

"I didn't think I would have a one-night stand either, but I did and look at me now." Liv muted the TV and looked at me. I watched as she fluffed her long brown hair and twirled a loose wave around her finger. "Who would have thought Xander and I would be—"

"Yeah, yeah, I get it," I said, cutting her off. I really wasn't in the mood to hear about how wonderful her relationship was with Xander, her boyfriend. Xander James was handsome, sexy, rich, and supposedly really good in bed—and with his tongue. I'd been hearing about Xander James for the last few months, and I just didn't get how one man could be so perfect. I was so happy for Liv; she was my best friend in the world, after all, but if I was honest, I was a bit envious as well. I wanted a guy who would sweep me off of my feet and fall head-over-heels in love with me. I wanted a guy who would look at me like I was the only woman on Earth. Right now, I got the guys who looked at me like I was a piece of discounted steak or like I was some sort of free entertainment. Hello, I'm not your personal stripper (unless you're dropping thousands of dollars and don't expect to be able to touch me), and no, I won't dress up in my high-school Hooters outfit for you (again). The fact was that Liv had hit the boyfriend lottery with Xander, and I was scraping the bottom of the barrel.

"Am I being annoying?" Liv frowned as she gazed at me, her brown eyes crinkling in concern that she was acting like that friend whom we all love to hate. That friend who finds her man, falls in love and can't stop going on and on about it. I didn't mind her going on about it normally. I just didn't want her to talk about her love life in the same breath as Aiden's name. Not when he was someone I'd been craving for years.

"No, Liv." I smiled widely, though inside I was grumbling that *yes, she was being annoying.* No one wanted to hear about their best friend's perfect lover every day. Though I suppose I was being unfair, since Xander was really quite far from perfect. I smiled wickedly to myself as I thought about their relationship.

"What are you smiling about?" Liv's eyes narrowed, and she moved closer to me. "Is there something you're not telling me, Alice?"

"Maybe." I grinned and started laughing as she sat there staring at me with a perplexed expression. I started to feel guilty when Liv's face started to look worried. I knew then that she was starting to feel bad and most probably overthinking everything. That was Liv's biggest failing and one of the reasons that I loved her. She was way too sensitive. She took on every emotion, and she was always super worried and anxious if she thought she was causing pain to anyone. "I'm just joking, Liv." I leaned forward to squeeze her arm. "I'm happy for you and Xander. You deserved to find love."

"I know." She smiled and then sighed. "But I want you to find love as well. I want you to be as happy as I am."

"I'll meet someone soon. I mean, we can even go out tomorrow night if you're down. I might meet a nice guy."

"Xander says he doesn't want me to go to any nightclubs with you anymore." She bit her lower lip, and I stared at her.

"I know that you aren't allowing Xander to dictate what you do and don't do, right?" I frowned. How dare he ban her from going to nightclubs with me, like I was some sort of bad influence?

"Of course not." She giggled. "We just can't announce it to him."

"You're not going to lie to him, are you?" I made a face. If she lied and he found out, he would hate me.

"No, of course not. I'm just not going to volunteer where we're going."

"Really?" I looked at her face carefully and then I saw the glint in her eyes. "You're such a liar, Liv. You're going to totally tell Xander, and then you're going to have him tell Aiden, and it's going to be all World War III up in the club and we're going to be banned for life."

"Just call him, Alice," she groaned. "Please."

"No." I shook my head and stood up. "I'm going to get some ice cream. Do you want anything?"

"No." She jumped up as well. "Why won't you call him? You're just being silly. Explain to him that you didn't want to kiss Scott."

"I'm not calling him." My face reddened as I remembered the look in Aiden's eyes when I'd kissed his brother a couple of months ago. He'd looked shocked, and I'd felt my stomach drop as our eyes met. It was just my luck. I hadn't even wanted to kiss Scott, but I'd let him kiss me, just so I could see if there was a spark. I wanted to explain to Aiden that it had been a mistake, but I was too ashamed to tell him anything. Especially given our past history together.

"Alice," Liv sighed and pursed her lips.

"Don't 'Alice' me, Liv." I rolled my eyes at her, starting to feel frustrated. "You wouldn't have called, either."

"Maybe not." She shook her head at me, and we both paused and looked down at her pocket as her phone rang.

"Get it." I walked away from her. "Your obnoxious Prince Charming is waiting for you."

"He's not obnoxious," she protested as she pulled her phone out of her pocket. And then she giggled. "Well, maybe he's slightly obnoxious," she admitted and then answered the phone. "Hello," she said softly in her 'I'm a princess, come and save me' voice, and I hurried down the corridor and into my bedroom.

I GRABBED MY LAPTOP, JUMPED onto my bed and pulled up Facebook. I typed 'Aiden Taylor' quickly in search and my heart froze as unfamiliar photos popped onto the screen. Had Aiden unfriended me? I swallowed hard, my heart beating fast as I refreshed the page.

"Oh my God," I groaned as I realized I'd typed in 'Tyler' instead of 'Taylor.' I quickly backspaced and deleted and changed it to the correct spelling. I felt a huge rush of relief escape me as Aiden's familiar photo crossed my screen. I clicked on his photos to see if he had any new pictures, and my heart stopped again when I noticed some girl called Elizabeth Jeffries had left a comment that said, "Can't wait to see you this weekend." I clicked on her name, but her profile was private and I couldn't see anything else.

Who the hell was Elizabeth Jeffries? Was she his girlfriend? Did he love her? Ugh! My head was spinning with questions as my stomach churned. I quickly went to Google and typed her name in and looked to see if I could find anything else about her online. That was what I hated and loved about the internet. It was so easy to stalk—I mean, "research"—people, but the flipside of that was that people could research me, too. I wasn't happy with the fact that when people typed 'Alice Waldron' into Google, a photo I'd submitted to a weight loss competition came up on a weight loss website, along with my goal weight (which I had not reached). I also wasn't proud of the fact that you could also see my posts on a celebrity gossip blog rating different Hollywood celebrities. I'd contacted Google and asked them to remove those websites from search, but they hadn't responded.

"Alice, what are you doing?" Liv walked into my room with two different tops in her hands.

"Research," I mumbled as I looked up at her, debating whether or not I should ask her if she knew who Elizabeth Jeffries was.

"Research for what?" Liv plopped down onto my bed, and I tried to adjust my laptop so that she couldn't see it. It was one thing to be a stalker, but it was another thing to be caught stalking. Especially when it involves your best friend's brother.

"Work," I lied and avoided her thoughtful gaze.

"What do you have to research for work?" she questioned, her voice doubtful. And who could blame her? I was an assistant at a real estate firm. There wasn't much that I did in the office, let alone had to do from home.

"What are you, an FBI agent?" I snapped, feeling peeved that she was questioning me.

"Okay, so what has Aiden been up to recently?" She laughed and I looked up at her. "I'm not dumb, Alice. I obviously can guess that your research is about my big bro. You've never had to do research for work before. Not that you've mentioned to me, anyway."

"Boo to my easy job." I laughed and handed my laptop over to Liv. "Do you know who Elizabeth Jeffries is, by any chance?"

"Elizabeth who?" she asked in a confused voice.

"I'm guessing that's a no." I sighed. "Do you know if Aiden is dating anyone?"

"Not that he's told me." She frowned. "Why? Does it say he's in a relationship on Facebook?"

"Not exactly." I shook my head. "But this whore Elizabeth is commenting on his wall."

"What? A prostitute?" Liv's eyes widened and she looked down at the computer to see what I was talking about. "How do you know she's a working girl?"

"Oh," I said meekly, feeling bad for calling my unknown nemesis and enemy a whore. "I don't know if she's really a whore, Liv. Keep up." I rolled my eyes at her.

"What?" She looked up at me. "You're confusing me. Is my brother dating a whore or not?"

"Oh my gosh, Liv," I groaned. "I was looking at Aiden's profile on Facebook and some *girl* called Elizabeth commented on his wall saying she can't wait to see him this weekend, and I called her a whore because I'm jealous and *I* want to see him this weekend," I explained feebly. "And if you didn't have your head in the clouds, you would have understood what I was talking about."

"Oh, I get it." She giggled. "She's not a whore, like she's hooking up for money, but she's a whore in that she's a ho because she's after your man."

"I prefer my explanation." I giggled. "Yours makes me sound like a psycho. I can't call her a ho because she's after my man because he's not my man."

"Alice," she groaned, "you're super confusing me."

"You're super confusing *me*." I made a face. "Now do you know her or not?"

"I've never heard of her before in my life," Liv said and handed me back the laptop. "Do you want me to call Aiden and see what's up?"

"I don't know. Do you think that will be obvious?" I asked her as I gazed down at Aiden's profile again. "Oh shit," I groaned out loud as I gave Elizabeth's comment a like. "I just liked her post on his wall. What should I do?"

"Unlike it quickly," Liv said as she shook her head. "And then like a different post, so if Aiden gets notifications, he will see you have a like somewhere."

"Ugh, he's going to know I was Facebook-stalking him." I sighed. "I'm such a loser."

"Alice, it's fine." She jumped off of the bed. "I'm sure he won't think anything of it."

"You think so?"

"I know so. Guys don't analyze Facebook likes and comments like we do." She smiled at me encouragingly. "He most probably won't even notice that you liked anything."

"Yeah, I guess so." I nodded hesitantly, my heart racing in fear. Liv was talking as if she knew what she was talking about, and she most probably thought she knew everything about men now that she was dating Xander, but I knew that she didn't really know that much. I mean, she hadn't been dating Xander for very long, and I was the one who had given her all her dating advice up until she started dating him. So essentially, Liv was giving me the advice I would have given her, and in all honesty, I had absolutely no idea what I'd been talking about when I was the one giving advice.

HAVE YOU EVER DONE SOMETHING you know you shouldn't do? Like sending a guy a Facebook message in the middle of the night, when you knew you absolutely should not be sending him a message? And doing it sober, no less. Drunk messaging and drunk dialing can be forgiven, but sober messaging is done by fools, like me.

I knew I shouldn't send Aiden a message. I knew I should wait for him to contact me. That's what all the rules say, right? If a guy is interested, he'll contact you. I knew that, but I was worried that he would think I had something for Scott—his brother. He caught me kissing Scott. Well, really he caught Scott kissing me, but ever since that night, Aiden has acted like I'm a leper or invisible. And I don't even *like* Scott, which he should know, but you know men. They can be weird and stupid and totally obnoxious and arrogant, and so that was why I sent Aiden a Facebook message at 11 p.m.

Hi Aiden, it's me, Alice. Hehe, obviously as it's from my Facebook page. Just wanted to say Hi. So Hi. And then I hit send. And then I fell back on my pillow and groaned. Why oh why had I sent a Facebook message to Aiden? Ugh. Then I heard a small ding and sat up again. Someone had sent me a message. I quickly looked at my Facebook account.

Hi Alice. That was all Aiden had said in his reply, but I felt as giddy as a drunk mouse as I stared at the screen. He had replied to me. He didn't hate me! I quickly clicked on my profile to see what photo I had up as my profile photo. I groaned as I saw myself grinning like a fool, my medium-length blonde hair looking messy and my blue eyes squinting. This was not the photo I wanted Aiden to be staring at as he typed back to me.

You're up late, I typed back quickly. I know, I know, I really shouldn't have sent another message. He hadn't exactly been enthusiastic in his response, but I didn't care. The fact that he had responded, period, was good enough for me.

It's 11pm. Not exactly last call. I rolled my eyes at his response.

I don't go drinking every night, so I wouldn't know, I typed back quickly. *Asshole.*

Just a few times a week? Only when Brock and Jock are available?

Haha. Very Funny. I made a face. Brock and Jock were twins that I had hired to pose as boyfriends for Liv and me in order to make Xander jealous when things hadn't been going too well for them. It hadn't worked out very well, and Brock and Jock hadn't fooled anyone into believing that they were our boyfriends.

What are you doing up so late? Looking to get into trouble? My heart stopped as I read his words. Was he trying to pick me up?

What kind of trouble? I typed back quickly.

You tell me.

What are you asking me, Aiden?

Nothing. I was just joking.

Oh okay. What are you doing?

About to hit the sack. I have a big meeting at work tomorrow.

Oh okay. Disappointment filled me. Tonight wasn't going to be the night that Aiden Taylor professed his love for me.

Aiden: *Sweet Dreams, Alice. Don't do anything I wouldn't do.*

Alice: *That might be hard.*

Aiden: *I'm well aware of that. :)*

Alice: *What does that mean?*

Aiden: *What do you think it means?*

Alice: *I'm not 16 anymore.*

Aiden: *I'm glad to hear it.*

Alice: *It was an honest mistake.* I lied. It hadn't been a mistake at all.

Aiden: *I know. You told me.*

Alice: *I got confused about whose bed was whose.*

Aiden: *Sure you did.*

Alice: *What does that mean? Sure you did.*

Aiden: *Alice, sweet dreams.*

Alice: *We should talk about this Aiden. I don't want you thinking anything that you shouldn't be thinking.*

Aiden: *That was a long time ago, Alice. I'm over it.*

Alice: *Fine. Good Night.*

I closed my laptop and jumped out of bed, feeling antsy. What did he mean he was over it? Was he still mad at me? Was he angry? Was he trying to tell me that he was over me and letting me know that I had no shot with him? I groaned as I walked to the kitchen and heard Liv and Xander whispering and doing heaven knows what in the living room.

"Get a room, guys!" I shouted into the living room with a snarl, suddenly feeling upset and angry at the both of them.

"Alice?" Liv sounded surprised, and I heard her get up off of the couch and walk into the kitchen. "Everything okay?"

"I'm fine. Just wondering why you guys think it's okay to make out in our joint living room," I said churlishly as I opened the fridge. "Isn't your boyfriend a millionaire or something? Do you guys have to make out in our living room, like some randy teenagers?"

"We weren't making out," Liv said simply. "We were watching a movie."

"So why did I hear whispering and kissing?"

"You heard kissing?" Liv raised an eyebrow at me. "Xander asked me to pass him the popcorn, and I told him to get his own," she explained and studied my face. "What's going on, Alice?"

"Nothing." I bit my lower lip, my face hot with shame. "Sorry."

"There's nothing to be sorry about." She continued to stand there. "Are you sad about Aiden?"

"He's just a jerk," I groaned again as I pulled out the carton of chocolate milk. "I don't know why he gets to me so much."

"Because you like him." She smiled.

"Yeah, I guess so." I poured a tall glass and then looked for some cookies. My stomach was in knots and I needed a sugar high to make me feel better.

"It's fine, Alice," she continued. "He's just being an ass. He'll come around, and he'll forget that silly little kiss."

"That's not everything," I said softly as I pulled out my purple box of Cadbury Fingers. They were my expensive treat to myself. They were more expensive than regular cookies because they were imported from England, but I loved my sticks of biscuit covered by milk chocolate. They were worth going broke for.

"What do you mean, that's not everything?" Liv stood behind me and as I turned around, her brown eyes looked cautious. "You didn't have sex with Scott, did you?"

"What?" My voice rose and my jaw dropped. "Hell no. Of course I didn't sleep with Scott. How could you think that?"

"Well, you're acting funny," she said with a frown. "What else don't I know, Alice?"

"Ahem." Xander walked into the kitchen and cleared his throat. "I've put the movie on hold, but I'm wondering if I should just leave?" He looked at me and then at Liv. "It seems like you guys need to talk?"

"Thanks." I nodded and smiled at him weakly.

"No." Liv frowned and then gave me a look. "You don't have to leave."

"Are you sure?" He stood there with a smug smile on his face. "I don't mind, and it seems like Alice really needs to talk." He looked at me again, and I stood there with my heart in my throat. I couldn't look at Liv. I was scared she was going to tell Xander he could stay. Which would mean that she was officially choosing him over me. Which would not be cool. I was her best friend. I had first dibs on her time. If she told him he could stay, I was going to feel very, very sad.

"If you don't mind," Liv said and walked over and gave him a kiss on the cheek. "I'll make it up to you." My shoulders relaxed at her words. She wasn't choosing Xander over me. Yet.

"I'll hold you to that," he said in a silky smooth voice, and I looked away as he pulled her mouth to his and kissed her firmly. Oh how I wished Aiden would grab me like that and kiss me possessively. "Feel better, Alice."

"Thanks." I nodded and chugged my chocolate milk.

"Alice, I'm going to walk Xander to the door then I'll be back." Liv looked at me. "Pour us two glasses of Merlot. I think tonight's going to be a long night."

"Okay." I nodded and smiled. I wasn't sure how I'd gotten so lucky as to get Liv as a best friend, but I vowed to myself that I would never take her for granted. I looked in the cupboard for some wine glasses and a bottle of wine. I then opened the fridge and took out some French bread and brie that I had not bought, and sliced the bread and put it in the mini toaster oven that we had. A couple of minutes later Liv walked back into the kitchen, and I tensed slightly. I was worried that she was going to be mad at me for making her send Xander home.

"Yummy, you're toasting the French bread?" She sidled up next to me and grinned.

"Yup, and I took out the brie, too." I looked over at her. "I hope that's okay."

"Of course." She laughed. "I got chocolate as well."

"Yay."

"It's dark, so it's good for us." She pulled out her bar of chocolate from the fridge. It was Lindt dark chocolate with mint, and I grinned. It was the only dark chocolate I liked because it didn't taste all gritty and bitter. The mint in this bar made the chocolate taste creamy and delicious. Almost as sinful as real milk chocolate.

"I'm sorry I made you send Xander home." I made a face as I turned the slices of French bread over so that they could be toasted on both sides. Our toaster was poorly made and it never seemed to toast the bread evenly on both sides.

"It's fine." She rubbed my shoulder. "I'm not going to just let you suffer; besides, he knows us both well enough to know that I couldn't just sit there while you were upset. He knows you're my best friend and—love it or hate it—he has to deal with it."

"He hates me?" I opened the fridge and pulled the butter out.

"No." She shook her head and laughed. "I think he hates—well, not *hates*, more like dislikes the fact that when we're together we can be a bit immature."

"Immature?" My jaw dropped. "He thinks I'm immature?"

"He thinks we're both a bit childish." She giggled. "I told him he was wrong, but you have to admit we do have a tendency to act like teenagers sometimes."

"I take offense to that." I laughed and then shook my head. "And it's not all the time, it's just sometimes."

"That's what I told him. Everyone is entitled to act young when they want."

"Exactly, and we're only twenty-two." I placed the bread on a plate with the cheese. "I'll take the food and you can bring the wine and the glasses."

"Okay." She nodded in agreement and followed me into the living room. I have to admit I felt bad when I saw the lit candles on the coffee table, with Liv's favorite cream faux angora wool blanket thrown on the couch. There was also a single red rose on the table next to the candle.

"Oh, man." I looked back at her with an apologetic look. "I ruined a romantic night."

"It's fine." She smiled at me.

"He gave you a red rose?" My heart had a sudden ache. "That's so sweet."

"He said that he's never given a woman a red rose before," she said, nodding. "He said that he vowed never to give a woman red roses until he met the woman he loved."

"Oh my God, that is so sweet." I sighed. "Argh, why does he have to be so perfect?"

"He told me that he couldn't believe that he was so lucky," she squeaked out with a huge grin. "He told me that I made him a believer and that he doesn't want to spend a day or night without me."

"Wow, thanks for making me feel even worse," I groaned. "How sweet is he?" I sighed. "I shouldn't have made him leave. Call him and tell him to come back. We can talk tomorrow."

"No, we will talk tonight." She sat down on the couch and opened the bottle of wine. "I want to know what's going on, Alice."

"It's not important. Call Xander and tell him to come back so that you can have hot sex and tell him you don't want to spend a night without him either."

"Alice." She giggled. "He can go without sex for one night. Might make him miss me even more."

"You're silly." I giggled. "Though, what's that saying? 'Treat them mean, keep them keen'?"

"'Make them wait, get the hate'?" she said with a laugh.

"Or 'Give them blue balls, get eaten by Jaws,'" I said.

"No, no, I've got it!" She laughed. "'Make them jack off, make them cough.'"

"Cough? Eh?" I started laughing harder. "That makes no sense."

"Make them cough up a big diamond ring." She laughed and I watched as her head fell back and her eyes watered up in tears.

"That's stupid!" I continued laughing and sipped at my wine. "But thanks for making me laugh."

"Of course." She grinned and then looked me directly in the eyes. "Now tell me, what haven't you told me?"

I took another sip of wine, swallowed and took a deep breath. "I lost my virginity to Aiden," I said softly, and I watched as Liv spat her wine onto her lap in shock.

TWO

There's no such thing as a love spell

YOU KNOW THAT SAYING. THE one about a watched phone never rings? Well, it's not true. My phone has been ringing off the hook all morning. The only person who hasn't called me is the one person I want to call me. I've had calls from the local satellite company telling me I needed to switch from cable. I told them I'll switch if they can promise that I only have to pay a dollar a month for the next ten years. She cursed at me and then hung up when I told her I wanted a new 50" TV as well to sweeten the deal. I also had a call from my dentist. Well, his receptionist called to tell me that I'd missed my last two appointments and that I needed to come in for a cleaning. Yeah, right. Not anytime soon, Dr. Rosenberg. The last time I needed a cleaning, I had several cavities that needed to be filled. I'm still paying off that bill. Thanks for nothing, $300-a-month insurance premium. And of course, I also had a call from my dear old grandma, wanting to know when I was getting married and giving her great-grandbabies. I told her she can go to the local park and see some babies there, but she wasn't amused.

So yes, I've had a lot of calls today, but none from Aiden, the man I really wanted to hear from.

Aiden Taylor is Liv's oldest brother. I've known him since I was a little kid, and I've had a crush on him since I was ten and he was sixteen. Not that he ever gave me the time of day. I was always his annoying kid-sister's best friend. Well, almost always. There was one time that I was more than that. One time that we shared a moment that I've relived every day of my life since it happened. Only it's not something I can talk about with him. Not at all. I'm lucky that he still talks to me after that little episode. And we're the only ones who know. Well, we were the only ones who knew. Until very recently. I didn't tell Liv at the time, and she's my best friend. I wanted to tell her. I really, really did, but how do you tell someone something like that? How do you tell your best friend that her brother was right, and that you're the bad influence that no one wants in their kids' lives? I guess I should be grateful that Aiden never said anything. I suppose he was embarrassed as well or something. I mean, it's not exactly something you shout out to the world. "Hey, Liv, I slept with your best friend. In fact, I took her virginity." Yeah, he didn't say that. And I didn't tell Liv, either. How could I tell her that I'd crept into her brother's bed with the hopes of seducing him? How could I tell her that we'd made love and that it had been the best night of my life? I didn't know how to tell her, and then I'd felt too guilty to bring it up, but now she knew and I honestly didn't feel better. I knew now that the one person I really needed to talk to about that night was the one man who wanted nothing to do with me.

"Alice!" Liv shouted as she walked into the apartment. "Where are you?"

"I'm in the living room!" I shouted back and then lowered my voice. "Why are we shouting by the way?"

"I've had a brilliant idea." Her eyes were sparkling as she ran into the living room. She clapped her hands and did a little dance as she grinned at me, her enthusiasm for her idea refusing to be quelled.

"What's the idea?" My eyes narrowed as she finally stood still.

"I have a way for you to start talking to Aiden again."

"Oh?" My heart raced at her words. I looked up at her and studied her face carefully. "A good idea or a harebrained idea?"

"Alice," she pouted, her eyes looking at me wickedly, "since when have I had harebrained ideas?"

"Since you became my best friend." I giggled and shook my head at her. Unfortunately it was true. We both seemed to have spur-of-the-moment ideas and plans that always seemed to get us into trouble. To be fair to Liv, I was the one who usually had the really stupid ideas, but Liv had been giving me a run for my money lately.

"We're going to join a flag football team."

"Say what?" I frowned.

"Flag football," she said excitedly. "Xander was telling me about it. He's going to be on it, too."

"Okay," I said, not feeling as excited. "How is this going to help me get Aiden?"

"He's going to be playing on the same team." She grinned. "It's going to be perfect."

"I don't know about this, Liv." I chewed on my lower lip. "Do you really think me playing football is going to win any guys? I'm not exactly the queen of anything sporty."

"Trust me." She grabbed my hands. "That's not the only plan I have. That's just step one."

"Step one?" I groaned, but my stomach was doing flip-flops in excitement. I wasn't a huge football fan, but if joining a team meant I would get to see Aiden weekly, then I was all for it.

"Oh yeah, baby." She grinned. "I've come up with a surefire way to make sure you and my brother get together." The look on her face looked so satisfied and excited that I held in my second groan. I didn't want to rain on her parade, but I'd also had a surefire plan once and it had blown up in my face.

"What's your surefire plan?" I asked weakly. There were times that I didn't love that I had rubbed off on Liv so much. When we were younger, Liv was innocent and quiet and I was the rabble-rouser, always looking to get into something. I always had a plan or a scheme, and they had never worked out as I'd planned them to.

"You're going to go to the flag football games with me and Xander. You're going to look pretty and flirt with all the attractive single men. You're going to be nice but not overly friendly to Aiden. You're going to let him see what he's been missing all these years."

"You think he's even going to care or notice?"

"I'm positive of the fact." She grinned. "Now that I know what happened between the two of you, I understand the dynamic between you both a lot better."

"Really?"

"Oh yes." She nodded. "I always wondered why he used to look at you with such protectiveness, but also with a kind of possessiveness and jealousy."

"He treats you the same way." I rolled my eyes, but my hopes were rising.

"Nope." She laughed. "Yes, he is overprotective and a bit of a jerk, but he's never acted jealous when I've talked about another guy and he's never acted possessive or upset when he's seen me with another guy. He couldn't care less. You know he told me he's glad I'm dating Xander because now Xander can worry about me."

"Yeah, but he's just saying that. He loves you."

"Yes, he loves me. I'm his sister." She grinned. "But he has feelings for you as well. Feelings that are about more than being your honorary big brother. I bet he's confused."

"Confused about what?"

"He's confused that he had this night with you all those years ago that he enjoyed, but feels guilty about it and now he's not sure what to do."

"You think so?" I asked hopefully.

"Yeah, I really do." She nodded. "The problem is he still sees you as a teenager. You need to show him you're a woman now."

"And flag football will do that?"

"You, in some short-shorts running down a field, with hot guys chasing you as your long blonde hair flies in the wind, will do that." She grinned again. "Come on, Alice, you know how guys are."

"But what about Scott? And what about my Facebook message?"

"Ah, forget them. They mean nothing."

"You think so?"

"I know so." She nodded.

"What do you know?" Xander's voice filled the room, and I groaned.

"What are you doing here?" I asked accusingly, and he laughed.

"Nice to see you too, Alice. I'm taking my girlfriend out to dinner. Is that okay with you?"

"Yeah, that's fine." I looked at Liv and she grinned.

"He was parking the car," she explained. "I left the door open for him to come in."

"Oh, okay. I was wondering if you gave him a key already."

"Would you have a problem with that?" Xander teased me. "I don't see anything wrong with that."

"I'm sure you wouldn't." I shook my head at him.

"I bet you wouldn't mind if Aiden had a key, though." He winked at me. "Maybe this time *he* can be the one to slip into *your* bedroom and bed."

"Liv!" I screamed as my face went hot. "You told Xander?"

"Xander!" Liv turned to him with angry eyes. "What were you thinking?"

"What?" he asked innocently.

"Why would you tell Alice that I told you?" She sighed and looked at me with apologetic eyes. "I'm sorry, but he wanted to know what was so important that I'd kick him out last night."

"So you told him?" My jaw dropped. "I can't believe you told Xander that I lost my virginity to Aiden."

"You had sex with Aiden?" Xander's voice sounded shocked, and my heart froze as I looked into Liv's eyes.

"You didn't know?" I frowned at him and then looked back at Liv.

"I didn't tell him everything." She sighed. "I didn't want to tell him everything. I just told him that you slipped into Aiden's bed one night and kissed him."

"Sex is a bit more than a kiss." Xander laughed and looked at me. "Well, well, well, Alice Waldron, the more I learn about you, the more intriguing you become."

"Argh. Whatever." I groaned and blushed again.

"Now I need to know exactly what went down." He laughed and looked at Liv. "And I thought *we* got together under crazy circumstances."

"Well, at least you guys *got* together." I sighed. "Aiden didn't give me the time of day after our night together."

"It wasn't exactly the same, though, was it, Alice?" Liv spoke softly. "I mean, he didn't know it was you at first."

"Don't remind me." I groaned and put my face in my hands. "I'm so embarrassed. I should just forget everything. There's no way that Aiden will ever be able to get past that incident."

"You never know," Liv said and beamed up at Xander as he kissed her cheek and rubbed her back. I wanted to gag at how lovey-dovey they looked. "What do you think, Xander?"

"I think I need to know exactly what happened." He looked at me and his green eyes turned from laughing to a more serious expression. "I know you might be embarrassed, but trust me: I can tell you if it's as bad as you think or if it's not as bad as you think."

"I'm just embarrassed." I looked down at the ground.

"It's not as bad as hooking up at a wedding with a stranger," Liv said.

"Yeah, it's not as bad as going back to a strange man's hotel room," Xander continued in a serious voice. "And then nicknaming him Mr. Tongue."

"Xander!" Liv hit him in the shoulder.

"Don't you mean 'Mr. Tongue?'" He grinned at her.

"I think she means Mr. *Miracle* Tongue." I laughed.

"Whatever." Liv blushed. "You're both gross."

"That's not what you said this morning," Xander said in a loud whisper, and she hit him harder.

"Shut up, Xander."

"You two!" I laughed. "Fine, I'll tell you what happened, but only because I want to know if you think I even have a chance. And if I should join the flag football team."

"Flag football team?" Xander frowned. "What?"

"Liv told me that Aiden is joining a team and that we should join."

"She what?" He turned to Liv. "You never told me that you wanted to join when I mentioned it earlier."

"Well, I didn't decide until recently."

"Uh huh, sure you didn't." He shook his head. "So you two are signing up?"

"Perhaps," I said at the same time as Liv.

"I don't know if this is a good idea, Liv." I shook my head. "I know you think it's a surefire plan, but surefire plans don't always work out."

"What's a surefire plan?" Xander narrowed his eyes and looked at Liv. "Liv?"

"Nothing." She smiled innocently. "I just want Alice and Aiden to interact on a weekly basis so that he can see what he's missing."

"Hmm," Xander said with a small frown.

"And she wants me to wear short-shorts," I added. "Which I don't think is a good idea."

"Short-shorts?" Xander laughed and shook his head. "That's your plan to get a man? Shake your ass in front of him?"

"I didn't know I was trying to get a man." Liv pursed her lips up at him. "But I guess I can wear short-shorts as well."

"Don't you dare," he said as he looked down at her ass for a few seconds. "Your big butt is mine and mine alone."

"My big butt?" Liv's voice dropped, and I grinned to myself. It was about to go down. Xander had no idea what he'd set into motion. Liv hated her butt, and I knew she did not consider his comment a compliment.

"Yeah,"—he slapped her ass lightly— "I like big butts."

"You what?" Her voice rose, and I swear daggers were flying from her eyes into his heart, stabbing him softly.

"I like big butts," he said and shrugged. "But your big butt is for me to enjoy, not every Tom, Dick and Harry on the football field."

"I do not have a big butt!" she squealed and immediately started doing squats. "Take that back."

"Take what back?" Xander looked confused, and I burst out laughing as Liv moved up and down with an annoyed look on her face. "Also, you're doing those squats all wrong. Your form is off."

"What?" she snapped.

"You shouldn't be bending your back like that. You should—"

"Shut up, Xander." She looked at me. "Can you believe he just told me I have a fat ass?"

"I cannot believe it." I looked at Xander. "Shame on you."

"What?" He threw his hands up with a confused look on his face. "I never said you had a fat ass. I said you had a big butt. A big butt that I like—love, even." He groaned at the murderous look on Liv's face. "Let me just shut up now."

"Yeah, you need to just stop." Liv stood up straight and stretched her arms out. "Ow." She made a face and looked at me. "My legs are aching."

"I'm not going to say you should work out more, then," Xander said with a smirk, and we both hit him on the arm. "Ouch, girls!"

"Alice, are you ready to tell my asshole of a boyfriend what happened with Aiden so we can all decide upon a plan of action?"

"Whoa, wait!" Xander frowned. "I'm not here to help you two come up with any spells or trickery, but more to give my advice."

"We're not witches. We don't cast spells or trick anyone." Liv rolled her eyes.

"You could have fooled me," he said with a straight face. "Brock and Jock?"

"Oh, get over them." Liv shook her head and looked at me. "Are you sure you want a boyfriend, Alice? Do you want to put up with all of this?"

"I wouldn't mind." I sighed wistfully and looked over at Xander. "I know you said he can be a pain, but sometimes it's nice to have a little pain."

"What have you been telling her?" Xander winked at Liv and she groaned.

"Not enough, obviously," Liv started up again and stopped herself. "Anyway, enough about you and me. Alice, I want you to talk about your story."

"Yeah, I guess," I groaned. "This is so embarrassing and almost unbelievable."

"Don't worry, Alice, there's nothing you can tell me that I wouldn't believe," Xander said. "And I've heard stories from Liv about the two of you, so trust me when I say that I can believe it all."

"Thanks." I made a face. "I'm not really sure that that's a compliment."

"Enough already," Liv said. "Xander is just looking to get himself into trouble."

"Okay," I said with a sigh and then closed my eyes. "I guess I should start at the beginning." I opened my eyes and looked at an expectant Xander and my face flushed as I opened my mouth to begin my story. The story of how I'd seduced Aiden Taylor, the older brother of my best friend in the world.

And then my phone rang. And my heart stopped beating for about three seconds as I stared. It was the call I'd been eagerly anticipating for the last six years. And I had absolutely no idea why he was calling.

THREE

*Sometimes a girl just
has to sneak into a bed*

I HAVE HAD A CRUSH on Aiden Taylor since I was ten. Yes, I know what you're thinking, how can you have a crush on a boy when you're ten and he is sixteen? Trust me, it is very, very easy. Aiden Taylor has always been handsome. And when he was sixteen, he was the stuff of every school girl's dreams. His now-dark hair had been a dirty blond then, and longer, almost like a surfer's, but he'd been on the baseball team. His bright blue eyes had always been full of mischief and he'd always treated me as an annoyance, just like he'd treated Liv, but I hadn't minded. In fact, I'd loved it. I loved spending time with him. I loved it when he let us play video games with him. I loved it when he'd tickled me or played board games with us. Aiden had been the bossy older brother, but he'd also made time to hang out with us. It had been easy to daydream about him becoming my boyfriend. Not that it was ever going to happen. I was too young for him, and he hadn't seen me as anything other than his sister's best friend. That was, until the summer after he'd graduated from college. He'd come home for the summer with his girlfriend, Lisa or something. I could still remember the first time we'd laid eyes on each other that summer. It had been a magical moment. I was sixteen, about to turn seventeen, and he was twenty-two. We hadn't seen each other for about two years, as his college schedule had kept him away except for holidays like Christmas, and even then he'd only been home for a few days.

Walking into the Taylor house that summer and seeing Aiden was like the first time you see a mountain or the ocean. It's a breathtaking, miraculous and awe-inspiring experience. But the walking into the house wasn't the best part. The best part was when Aiden looked at me. It was magical. It was one of those moments that you live to go through. Everyone should have a moment like that at least once in their life. I can remember it clearly. I'd walked into the living room, and he'd looked up casually to see who it was. And his eyes had lit up in appreciation for ten glorious seconds as he looked me up and down. In that moment, I'd been Alice Waldron, beautiful swan, and he'd taken in all of my glory. His eyes had met mine and for a few seconds, he'd smiled at me, with a flirtatious, sweet smile that had flipped my heart over a million times as if I were an Olympic gymnast. And then Liv had run into the room and given me a hug, and he'd become his old bossy self, acting as if he had been personally assigned as our warden and we were his inmates.

I'm not exactly sure how I came up with my plan. It wasn't something that I'd thought about for a long time. I hadn't spent my years plotting how to seduce Aiden Taylor. Not at all. I think it really came to me in the moment, out of jealousy and excitement. You see, it had killed me that

Aiden wasn't alone that summer. Especially as I knew that Lisa was beautiful and easy. Okay, I didn't know if she was really easy, but I assumed she was. Of course, she was sleeping in a separate bedroom, but that didn't stop them from sneaking off and making out—something that had made me extremely jealous. Then one night, Lisa had given me a note and asked me to give it to Aiden. Of course, I'd opened it and read it. And of course, I'd seen red as I read it furiously. Lisa had stated that she was going to sneak into Aiden's bedroom that night at midnight. She told him to keep the lights off and to have protection ready. She said she didn't want to disrespect his parents, but she needed him badly and didn't want to go another night without him. She also said, which made me smile, that she was sad that he didn't think their relationship was going to work out and that she still loved him, even if he was technically no longer her boyfriend. This made me grin for days. Of course, I'd seen them arguing, but I'd had no idea that they had broken up. That meant I still had a chance. Of course, I was conveniently forgetting that I was in high school still and he had just graduated from college. That seemed to be of no real importance to me. You should know that I did hand Aiden the note. And he screwed it up in his hand and threw it into the trash. I did what I thought I should do, and I told Lisa that Aiden didn't want her to come to his room. She seemed upset, but accepted it calmly. I did feel a bit guilty as I heard her making a call for someone to pick her up. Though my guilt left when I saw a hot Tom Cruise lookalike arriving about thirty minutes later and kissing her like he'd been away at war and hadn't seen her in years. Lisa left so quickly that I felt bad for Aiden, as she hadn't even told him goodbye. Well, not really that bad. And I can't say that's exactly what gave me my idea, but it was definitely one of the reasons I thought I was pretty brilliant. My plan was pretty simple: I was going to sneak into bed with Aiden, and we were going to snuggle and kiss and I was going to seduce him. And it had worked. I'd snuck into his bedroom around midnight wearing nothing but a long T-shirt. I'd slipped into his bed and put my arms around his naked chest and pressed myself up against him.

"You shouldn't be here." He groaned sleepily as his fingers had grabbed mine.

"Shhh." I'd kissed his back, and ran my feet down his muscular legs. The hair on his legs had tickled my smooth skin, and I'd moaned at the feeling of being so close to him. His hand ran up and down the side of my legs and he'd groaned before turning over. The room had been pitch dark and as he rolled me onto my back and kissed me, I'd been scared that he'd figure out it was me and get mad. I was pretty sure that Aiden didn't know that Lisa had left because he had gotten home late that night and gone straight to his room. His tongue had entered my mouth swiftly, and I'd kissed him back with such ferocity that I'm sure he must have been shocked. He'd paused for a moment and pulled away from me and then whispered, "Damn, you shouldn't be here." I had grabbed his head and pulled him back down to me and wrapped my legs around his waist. At the time I'd thought he was talking to Lisa, but now—now I wasn't really sure if he'd known that he'd been talking to me, Alice. If he'd known it was me and he'd still gone ahead, that must mean something, right? That night had been crazy and passion-filled and when he'd entered me, I'd cried out in pain and ecstasy. He'd been the perfect lover: attentive, caring, dominating and skilled.

The next morning when I'd woken up, he was staring at me angrily. I can still remember the shock and disgust in his icy blue eyes. I'd gulped and blushed and hurried out of the bed, waiting for him to say something, anything, to let me know everything was going to be okay. But he'd said nothing. Not then and not ever. Not until recently. And now, well, now all I wanted to do was to repeat that night. But this time, I wanted to play for keeps. This time I wanted to seduce my best friend's brother and make him fall in love with me. And I was willing to do almost anything for that chance with him. And what I really meant was *whatever* it took.

"HELLO, ALICE?" HIS VOICE WAS hesitant and strong at the same time, and I felt as if time had stood still. My fingers gripped the phone and my face grew warm as I realized that Aiden was on the other end of the line. I looked at Liv and mouthed, "Oh my God, oh my God" to her several times. "Alice?" he repeated again, and I shook my head, trying to get over my shock.

"This is Alice," I said in a prim voice, sounding like some Victorian matron from an old black-and-white movie.

"It's Aiden," he said in a husky voice, and I swear to God that I would have started jumping up and down if Xander hadn't been sitting in the same room as me, looking very bemused.

"Who?" I said childishly, and I saw Xander rolling his eyes.

"Aiden Taylor, Liv's brother."

"Oh, hi, Aiden. How are you?" I said stiffly as I grinned at Liv who was grinning back at me. Xander was looking back and forth at our expressions with an even more bemused look, and I knew he was thinking to himself that it didn't take much to make us happy.

"I'm good." Aiden cleared his throat. "I was actually just calling to see if Liv is okay?"

"Liv?" I said stiffly. Huh? What was he talking about?

"Yeah, I tried texting her a couple of days ago, and she hasn't responded, so I figured I would check with you."

"She's fine," I said and put my finger up to my lips as I looked at Liv. "Hold one second, please," I said quickly and pressed mute. "It's Aiden. He said he's tried contacting you and you haven't answered," I whispered to Liv and she frowned.

"Uh, no." She shook her head. "What is he talking about? I just spoke to him this morning."

"Oh." I shrugged my shoulders. "So he's lying? Should I tell him you're here with me now?"

"Yeah." Liv nodded. "Tell him that I'm here and that I said I spoke to him this morning."

"Okay." I was about to unmute, when Xander shook his head and sighed.

"Do you two have absolutely no clue?" He stood up and walked toward me. "That's still on mute?"

"Yes." I nodded.

"Good." He stopped in front of me and his green eyes pierced mine. "Listen to me carefully. Do not tell Aiden that you know that he's lying. He obviously used that as an excuse to call you. You should be thanking your lucky stars, not accusing him of lying." He shook his head and looked back at Liv. "I have no idea where you are getting your advice from." He turned back to look at me. "Get back on the phone and ask him something. Be nice. Be sweet. Be happy to hear from him. Don't accuse him of lying. Don't have an attitude. Don't talk about kissing Scott or seducing him when you were sixteen. Stick to topics that are safe for now. Do you hear me?"

"Yes." I nodded meekly.

"I don't know why he's calling you," he said with a serious face. "Maybe he got hit in the head and actually likes you."

"Xander!" Liv screeched.

"I'm sorry." He laughed and looked at her. "But really, I think I got hit in the head as well."

"Why's that?" She frowned.

"'Cause I'm dating you." He grinned at her, and she just shook her head and mumbled something. "But you know I love you. That's why I'm letting you move in with me."

"What?" I froze and looked at Xander and then Liv's pink face. "You're moving in with Xander?"

"Oh, boy." He bit his lower lip and stepped back. "You didn't tell her?" He looked at Liv and she glared at him.

"I'm sorry, Alice. I was going to tell you. And it's not for—"

"We'll talk later." I made a face at her and then unmuted the phone. "Sorry about that," I sang into the phone, my heart racing as I thought about Liv moving out.

"That's okay," Aiden said stiffly. "Where did you go?"

"I had another call," I lied. "I just got asked out on a date."

"Oh?"

"Yeah, this guy I met last weekend. His name is Sylvester," I said and I could see Xander rolling his eyes as if he couldn't believe I was going down the lying road again.

"Sylvester Stallone?" Aiden asked and I laughed.

"Funny—not," I said. "I didn't say Rambo called me."

"That's good. I don't think I can take Rambo on."

"Oh?" My heart felt as if it were going to pop out of my chest then. What did he mean he couldn't take Rambo on? Did that mean he liked me? Did he want to date me? My stomach was doing somersaults.

"Yeah." He laughed. "He might not like you getting calls from guys, even if they're just friends."

"Oh yeah," I said, suddenly deflated. "That's true."

"Anyway, I also just wanted to see if you were okay."

"Okay?"

"After our Facebook chat the other day," he said softly. "I wasn't sure if I'd upset you."

"Why would I be upset?" I squeaked out.

"I realize we've never really spoken about that night," he said awkwardly. "And I wanted to apologize for what happened."

"You wanted to apologize to me?" I said stiffly. The moment felt surreal, and then the room started to spin. How was it that he was calling to talk about that night just when I was talking about that night as well?

"I should have known better." He sighed. "I shouldn't have let it continue once I knew."

"Once you knew what?" I said softly, my face burning in shame.

"Once I knew it was you in my bed."

"You knew?" My jaw dropped. "Before the morning?" Excitement and hope ran through my veins at his words.

"Of course I knew, Alice." His voice was husky. "How could I not have known?"

"But ..." My voice trailed off. "I didn't know you knew before the morning."

"I wasn't proud of myself." He sighed. "But yes, I knew." He cleared his throat. "I knew as soon as you got into the bed and wrapped your arms around my chest. Actually, I knew as soon as you walked into the bedroom. I could smell your strawberry fragrance hanging in the air as soon as the door opened."

"I, uh—I don't know what to say," I squeaked out. I had loved that strawberry spray and the matching strawberry lotion. I'd worn them both so much that my mom had asked me if I wanted to move to a strawberry patch.

"I shouldn't have brought it up. I just wanted to make sure you were okay," he said softly. "I know we're older now and we had some awkwardness recently, but I wanted to reach out and let you know that I consider you a part of the family, Alice, and I hope you know that."

"Thanks," I said softly, my head spinning. I was so confused. Why was he calling me? Did he like me or not? And what did he think about that night we'd spent together? Did he ever think about it? And did he ever think about me? Did he wish that he could have another night with me? Or did he wish that he could have many more nights with me?

"Anyway, I should go now," he said cheerfully. "Tell Liv to text me back or call me when you see her. I hope to see you soon."

"Where are you going?" I said, knowing I sounded pitiful, but I didn't want the conversation to end.

"I have a date," he said. "I'm taking her to a Degas exhibit." He groaned. "Don't I sound boring?"

"No," I said lightly as my heart lurched.

"You're too sweet, Alice," he said, his voice sounding sexy as hell. "I just hope Elizabeth enjoys it."

"Elizabeth Jeffries?" I said, unable to stop myself.

"Yes, how did you know?" He sounded surprised.

"Good guess," I said and then sighed. "But I have to go. Talk to you soon."

"Oh, okay. Bye, Alice," he said softly, and I hung up. I looked at Liv and Xander and I knew that I looked like a sad case because that was how I felt— really sad and sorry for myself.

"What's wrong?" Liv jumped up and ran toward me. "What did my brother say? God help me, but I'll kill him if he was a jerk."

"He has a date," I said softly, my voice cracking.

"You did just tell him another guy had called you," Xander said and closed his mouth as Liv glared at him.

"Oh, no." She rubbed my shoulder.

"And he knew it was me that night." I rubbed my forehead and then sank down into the couch. "He knew it was me before the next morning," I said again in a daze. "I can't believe it." I shook my head and my mind went back to that night six years ago, the night that had been both the best and worst in my life. The night that I was determined to experience again. Only this time I was a woman and I sure wasn't going to sneak out of the room the next morning with anything other than a grin and a well-loved body.

"So what are you going to do?" Liv said, her eyes wide with shock.

"I don't know," I groaned. And I really wasn't sure. "I guess I'll start by joining the flag football team."

"Hold that thought, I'm going to get us some drinks." Liv jumped up and hurried out of the living room. I nodded at her and sat back and closed my eyes, my heart still thudding from my call with Aiden.

"So I need to talk to you." Xander moved closer to me on the couch as Liv left the room. My heart raced as his voice lowered, and I felt him next to me. What was he doing? Was he going to make a move on me? What sort of woman did he think I was? Did he really think I was going to let him come on to me when he was dating my best friend?

"About?" I looked up at him warily, and his green eyes looked amused as he gazed at me. *Oh God, please don't tell me you want me to experience your miracle tongue as well, please do not make me have to slap you.*

"What are you thinking, Alice?" he said softly, a small smile on his face as I glared at him.

"Liv is my best friend, and I will tell her if you do anything inappropriate."
I made a face at him and then took a deep breath. "And then she'll leave you,
and you'll—"

"Alice." He cut me off as he rolled his eyes. He looked as if he wanted
to laugh at me. "I need to tell you something, and I don't want Liv to hear.
Not because I'm trying to hit on you, but because I don't want to make her
uncomfortable."

"Uncomfortable how?" I asked him suspiciously.

"It's about Aiden."

"What about Aiden?" I frowned and leaned forward as my heart raced.
What did he have to tell me about Aiden that he couldn't say in front of Liv?

"I think Aiden is a Dom."

"Say what?" My eyes widened as he spoke.

"I think Aiden is a Dominant."

"What?" I screeched as I stared at him. My face was reddening as I
thought about Aiden with a whip in his hand and me lying across his lap.
Wait, could that even work? And would I even want him to use a whip? I
chewed on my lower lip as my mind raced. Maybe I'd just be on his lap and
he could use his hand. Yes, that was preferable to a whip.

"A Dominant is someone who takes a superior position in the bedroom
and—" Xander interrupted my thoughts, and I blushed as a dart of
embarrassed heat spread through my body.

"I know what a Dom is." My face reddened. "I've been around town, you
know." Well, I've kinda been around town. I've never been with a guy that

was into much experimental play, not that I haven't tried, but, well, it's just never worked out for me.

"Okay, Alice," Xander answered me smugly.

"Why do you think he's a Dom?" I asked him curiously, my heart racing quickly again, this time in excitement. Had Aiden told Xander that he wanted me to be his submissive? I wasn't sure what I'd say to that. I'm not exactly the submissive type. I think I talk too much and I don't take orders well. In fact, I like to order men around. Especially in the bedroom; I like to let a man know what I want very clearly.

"Shh." Xander shook his head. "Keep your voice down. I don't want Liv to know."

"Why not?"

"Would you want to know if your brother was a Dom?"

"I don't have a brother." I shrugged.

"Would you want to know if Liv was a Dom or a sub?"

"She would tell me." I shrugged again and then grinned at him. "We share all of that information."

"Hmmm." He frowned for a second and then shook his head. "Well, I don't think that this is something Liv wants to think about her brother doing."

"What?" I laughed. "Spanking women?" I winked, and I was almost positive that I'd made Xander blush. I had said spanking on purpose, of course. Liv had told me that Xander had a penchant for giving her a quick spank before doing doggy-style, though I wasn't going to tell him I knew that. Not in an even more obvious way, anyway. I wasn't sure that he'd be happy knowing I knew intimate details about their sex lives. At least not if the frown on his face was any indication.

"I don't know what he does exactly." Xander grinned. "But it seems like you would be into that, huh?"

"Into what?" I frowned and looked down, not wanting him to see the eagerness in my face.

"The kinky stuff," he said with a light in his eyes. "Maybe that's a way for you to entice him," he said softly. "Let him know you're down for experimenting."

"Ooh." I nodded thoughtfully. Maybe Xander had a point. Maybe Aiden was being wary because he didn't know if I'd be interested in getting down and dirty in all sorts of different ways. Maybe I needed to show him I could be a sub. Not that I'd make a great one, but I could try. And maybe I could be a great one. I was great, after all. And I had skills. Though, I didn't know if the skills I had were the sorts of skills I needed to be a sub. I wondered what I would have to wear as a sub. Would he have me in leather chaps? Would he expect me to wear nipple clamps? I cringed as I thought about the pain I'd feel wearing nipple clamps. The sex had better be good if I was going to wear nipple clamps. I'd have to look them up online or maybe even go to a sex store. I'd convince Liv to go with me. Maybe I could pick up a sexy outfit or some toys that I'd casually let Aiden see the next time I saw him. I could let some handcuffs fall out of my bag the next time I saw him or something.

"Alice, you okay?" Xander's voice sounded concerned, and I looked up at him with an apologetic smile.

"Sorry, I spaced out a little bit." I shook my head to clear my thoughts. I was getting carried away already. Even if it was only in my mind. I couldn't wait to speak to Liv about what Xander had told me. Though I wouldn't tell him that I was going to tell her. I'm not sure what Xander was thinking, but how could he possibly think I wasn't going to tell Liv? We told each other everything. There was no way I was keeping this to myself. I was going to let Aiden see that I could be the best sub he could ask for, and Liv was going to help me.

"That's okay." He looked at me uncertainly. "I hope I didn't shock you with the news."

"Oh, not at all." I smiled sweetly, my mind racing. Xander hadn't shocked me at all. In fact, he'd just given me the perfect idea to try and get Aiden once and for all.

FOUR

Master of the universe

GAME NIGHT AT THE TAYLORS' house was a tradition that had been
going on for years. What was funny about game night was that only Aiden
and Liv were interested in playing board games. Their parents never played,
Scott played sometimes, and Chett never played at all.

"I'm going to take you all down." Aiden wiggled his eyebrows as he
looked at Xander, Liv and me with a serious face and I tried not to laugh.
He was so far from intimidating when he made that face, but I knew he
wasn't joking. Aiden never joked about board games. He played to win, and
he pretty much always did.

I stared at Aiden's face for a few seconds and wondered how it was that
he could be so good looking without being completely cocky. Aiden Taylor
is classically handsome in the way that means that pretty much any woman
can look at him and find something to appreciate. That's not why I like him,
though. Yes, his eyes are vividly blue and remind me of the sky on a clear
summer day; yes, his hair is dark and silky with a slight curl that makes him
look dangerously sexy; yes, his lips are full and pink, and have a curl to them

that makes him look roguish; yes, his skin is a tan olive brown and his body is fit and muscular without looking like he's Mr. Universe ... Yes, I'm attracted to his looks, but what I like most about Aiden is the fact that underneath his bossy-older-brother persona, he is deeply caring, wickedly intelligent, and he has a secret naughty side to him that I love seeing come out. And even more than that, he's always been there for me even when I didn't know I needed him.

"Are you going to play, Alice?" Aiden asked me and poked me in the shoulder.

"Sorry, I was just thinking," I said and smiled at him as I picked up the dice. He smiled back at me and then looked away and started counting his money. I laughed at the happy look on his face. Aiden had always loved playing Monopoly, and he was the king of property buying. He always acted as if the game were real life and he was always a sore loser when he happened to lose a game, which had only happened once. And if I'm completely honest, I wasn't sure if he had lost on purpose or not.

"Thinking is not acting," he said with a stern face. "Roll the dice and move."

"See what I told you, Xander?" Liv said and kissed her boyfriend. "Aiden takes this game so seriously. He really thinks he is buying real properties and hotels."

"Don't be a sore loser, Liv," Aiden said, and Liv laughed.

"We just started playing ten minutes ago. You haven't won yet."

"Yet," he said with a smirk and then looked back at me. "Are you going to play?"

"I'm playing, jeez," I said and rolled the dice and then moved my piece. "I'm not buying the property," I said as I looked at my cash.

"What?" Aiden looked at me like I was crazy. "How can you not buy it? You always have to buy."

"I'm saving my money." I shrugged and adjusted the strap of my top as it was sliding off of my shoulder. I noticed Aiden's eyes shift from my face to my shoulder and his gaze became more intense as he watched me adjusting my bra strap as well. My fingers got stuck underneath the strap for a moment, and Aiden moved towards me. For a second I thought he was going to help me untangle my fingers, but he didn't. I released my breath, and he moved back.

"You can play now." I smiled at him sweetly. "My turn is done."

"That was a bad move," he said and shook his head. "How many times do I have to tell you and Liv to always buy a property?"

"I didn't want to," I said, and I saw Liv rolling her eyes as Xander smiled.

"Well, you should have," Aiden said and picked up the dice. "I know you like being difficult, Alice, but really you should listen to me when it comes to playing board games."

"I know, I know," I said and picked up my bottle of water. "You know best. You're the king of Monopoly, the baron of fake-property buying, the master of the universe."

"The master of the universe, huh?" Aiden smiled and licked his lips. "I don't know if I'm the master of the universe, but I can be a master of other things."

My breath caught, and I looked away as my face grew red. Was Aiden confirming what Xander had told me? There was no way that he knew that

I knew he was a Dom, so I wondered if he thought he was being smart. I stared at his hands and shivered slightly as I imagined them doing dirty things to me. Very, very dirty things.

"What other things?" I said softly and looked down at his belt. "Leather things?"

"Leather things?" His eyes caught mine, and I couldn't read his expression. "Okay, I'm buying Park Avenue." He changed the subject without continuing and I looked over at Liv, who was looking very confused. I really needed to talk to her about what Xander had told me. I knew it would be awkward for her to hear that her brother was a Dom, but my sanity was more important than her feeling awkward at this point.

"Get ready to pay me all of your money, bitches." Aiden sounded gleeful, and Liv gasped.

"Is that any way to speak to women?" she said tartly. "Bitches? Really, Aiden?"

"No." Aiden jumped up from the ground. "Sorry, girls, I got a bit carried away. My apologies to you two gentle damsels."

"I'm no damsel," I said and sipped some more water. "You don't need to be gentle with me."

"That's good to know." Aiden winked at me and studied my face for a few seconds. "Anyone want a beer or anything else from the kitchen?"

"I think I'll come with you and grab a beer." Xander jumped up as well. "Girls?"

"I'll have a Blue Moon, please. And some chips."

"I'll have a Blue Moon as well," Liv said. "And bring some more salsa out."

"Anything else, ma'am?" Xander teased her, and she stuck her tongue out at him.

"Yes, some popcorn too," she said as they exited the room. "Don't forget the popcorn."

"How could I forget the popcorn?" Xander looked at her from the door and then exited.

"What is going on?" Liv screeched as soon as they'd left the room.

"What are you talking about?" I said with a frown. "What do you mean, 'what is going on?'"

"You and my brother are flirting." She pointed a finger at me. "Master of the universe and damsel in distress?" She giggled as she studied my face. "What are you two going on about?"

"We're not flirting." I groaned. "I wish we were flirting. I wish he were interested in me."

"Alice, trust me. Aiden is flirting." She cocked her head to the side. "Why do I feel like there is something you haven't told me?"

"Liv," I whispered as I stared at the door. "You will not believe what I have to tell you."

"Oh my God, what?" She leaned forward eagerly.

"Xander told me ..." My voice trailed off and I lowered my voice some more. "You cannot tell him I told you."

"Oh my God, what did he tell you?" she said, her voice growing louder.

"Shhh, Liv!" I groaned. "Look, I don't have time to tell you now, but I will tell you later."

"You're killing me." She made a face. "I want to know now."

"I seriously can't tell you now," I said, and Liv frowned.

"Give me a clue, at least. You can't just leave me hanging."

"I'm not leaving you hanging," I said and then leaned forward. "Let me just say that Aiden likes to be in control."

"Huh?" Liv looked confused. "What does that mean?" Her eyes searched mine. "What do you mean he likes to be in control?"

"I mean he likes to be in control." I emphasized the last word and widened my eyes. I moved my hand back and forth in a quick slapping motion, but I could tell that Liv had no idea what I was acting out. The look on her face was one of deep confusion.

"Okay, here are the beers." Aiden walked into the living room then, and I blushed as I took the beer. Every time I looked at Aiden now, all I could think about was him spanking me or bossing me around in the bedroom. Unfortunately, I had no real clue what went on in a Dominant/submissive relationship, so I knew I was going to have to do some research if I was hoping to get him to believe that I was interested in being a part of that lifestyle.

"So who's up now?" Aiden said as he sat down and handed me a bowl of chips.

"Liv," I said with a smile, and we both turned to Liv who was busy kissing Xander. "You're up, Liv."

"Oh, sorry," she said with a small smile as she played with Xander's hair. I looked at the board and smiled to myself as we waited for her to play.

"Reminds me of old times," Aiden said softly, and I looked up at him with a small smile.

"Oh?" I said just as softly.

"Liv being preoccupied with a boy and us having to wait," he said and reached over to grab some chips. "Do you remember that night we played by ourselves?"

"I do," I said quietly, surprised he had remembered. "I was thirteen and you were eighteen," I said with a laugh. "And it was Valentine's Day."

"Yup." He nodded. "And you were so upset because Liv spent the whole night chatting to her friend on the phone."

"What friend?" Xander frowned, and Liv giggled as she punched him in the shoulder.

"I was thirteen." She shook her head. "His name was Lucas Johnson, and he was fourteen, and I thought we were going to get married and live happily ever after."

"Hmph," Xander said, and I smiled at his slightly jealous expression.

"They weren't even really dating," I said. "Liv just had a crush on him, and they spent most of their calls talking about wrestling."

"Ugh, and heavy metal." Liv made a face. "I don't know how he believed that I enjoyed listening to heavy metal."

"Heavy metal?" Xander looked confused.

"Liv told him she loved heavy metal and wrestling because he loved them and she wanted to connect with him." I giggled as I thought back to the silly lies we'd told as teenagers.

"Hey, he liked to talk about music," she said, defending herself. "I used to sing that one Guns and Roses song every time I saw him."

"Knock, Knock, Knocking on Heaven's Door!" At the same time we both sang out loud the title of the only Guns and Roses song that we knew and then burst into laughter.

"I guess you've both been a bit immature for a long time, then?" Xander asked in an amused tone as he gazed at Liv lovingly.

"I wouldn't say immature," I said defensively, thinking about my current plan to try and seduce Aiden.

"Yeah, we're not immature," Liv said and punched Xander in the arm again. "We're just fun-loving."

"Uh huh," Aiden said and shook his head, his eyes never leaving my face. I looked up at him, and I wondered what he was thinking. He had a half-smile on his face, and I wanted more than anything to be able to lean forward and just kiss him. I let out an involuntary sigh, and I watched as Aiden's eyes dropped to my lips and then back up to my eyes. A sharp thrill ran through my stomach and the room went quiet. I felt tense and excited and I could barely breathe. The electricity between us was tangible and I waited with bated breath for Aiden to say something else.

"Back to my story." He grinned. "Remember how I saved you from eternal depression and disappointment?"

"Hmmm, eternal depression and disappointment, eh?" I raised an eyebrow at him, but my heart was thudding. I could remember that night as if it were yesterday. It was one of the moments between us that reminded me why I'd fallen so hard for him.

I'd been thirteen and a bit awkward. In fact, both Liv and I had been awkward. We'd been average students, both with braces and slight acne. We weren't cool kids and we weren't really smart, either. We'd been just normal teenage girls: a bit goofy, really into boys, really into talking about boys and really into wishing boys would notice us. Liv had invited me over for a slumber party on Valentine's Day, but had gotten a call about ten minutes after I'd arrived, and I'd sat in the Taylors' living room watching TV with her parents and feeling sorry for myself. Scott and Chett were out, and Aiden was busy studying for some test. At thirteen I'd already felt like a bit of a loser, and I'd been so excited when Aiden had seen me sitting with his parents watching *Jeopardy* and asked if I wanted to be his Valentine's date. Now, he hadn't meant in a romantic sense—I'd been thirteen and he'd been eighteen—but he'd wanted to cheer me up. Of course, I'd eagerly said yes. I mean, Aiden was a like a Greek god to me, so hot and so untouchable. I'd jumped off of the couch so fast and we'd gone into the kitchen and to the games' cupboard. He'd pulled out Monopoly (his favorite game) and asked me if I wanted to share a pizza. Of course, I'd said yes, even though his parents had already fed me lasagna. Aiden had taken a frozen pizza out of the freezer, and poured us each a glass of orange Sunkist. We'd sat at the kitchen table and played Monopoly all night. I'd felt like a million bucks; especially after he'd made strawberries dipped in chocolate for me. That was perhaps the first time I'd ever thought of Aiden in a truly romantic way. My heart had soared at how caring he was being. I could still remember the words he'd said to me as I'd complained to him that I was afraid I'd be alone forever. Liv had a valentine and had left me to just watch TV with his parents, and I'd had no one. He hadn't laughed and told me I was too young to have such worries. He hadn't called me a loser. He hadn't made comments about me being thirteen and too young for love. No, he'd smiled at me and picked up my hand and leaned forward and looked deeply into my eyes. His voice had been deep as he spoke and told me that "one day I would meet a guy that would make me feel like the only girl on the world. One day I wouldn't care about Valentine's Day because every day of my life would feel special. That the man that I ended up with would be worth the wait and that I should never settle for anything less than true love." He'd then stroked the top of my head and told me that one day I'd meet the right guy, the guy made especially for me and that nothing would be more important to me than that guy. In that moment, I'd known deep in my heart that he was that guy. I hadn't said anything of course, since I knew he just saw me as his sister's best friend. I knew that I was someone he cared for, but I was still a little kid; deep inside, though, I'd known: *he* was that guy for me. The moment hadn't lasted long because he'd let go of my hand within seconds and gone back to playing Monopoly and telling me off for not upgrading my houses to hotels, but I hadn't minded. The fact that Aiden had spent his Valentine's Day trying to make me feel better and special had meant more to me than anything in the world. It meant that I could put up with his superior attitude when we played Monopoly because I knew deep inside that while Aiden was bossy and arrogant, he had a heart of gold and he cared about me and my feelings. I knew that he was a guy who I could always count on; even if for him, I was just his sister's best friend.

"Alice, it's your turn again." Aiden's voice distracted me from my thoughts, and I blinked slowly as I gazed at him, momentarily forgetting I was twenty-two and not still thirteen.

"Sorry," I said softly and picked up the dice and rolled them gently. I wondered if he remembered our conversation from that night. I wondered if he remembered how he told me to wait for Mr. Right. I wondered if he knew that I thought he was the one. I wondered what he would think if he knew of the plans I had for the two of us. I sighed inwardly as I thought of those plans. A part of me told me to just be patient and let fate play its hand, but the other part of me was too impatient to wait any longer.

FIVE

Not all athletes are in shape

HAVE YOU EVER EXPERIENCED THAT emotion that feels like it could become tears or laughter in the same moment? It's like your head can't quite decide how you want to express your feelings. Seeing Aiden at flag football practice, the week after game night, in his black shorts and skintight white T-shirt was one of those moments for me. I was so overwhelmed by emotions that for a few seconds I felt as if the air had been punched out of me.

"Alice, what are you doing?" Liv pushed me forward as I'd just stopped moving in the middle of the field.

"Aiden," I said weakly as my knees started to crumble. My heart was racing and my face was burning. I have to admit I felt like I was ten again and seeing my childhood crush, Tommy Walker, sitting in my English class flipping his long blond surfer-like hair.

"You're doing Aiden?" Liv laughed at me. "Say what?" she said as she stared at me and giggled. "Are you okay?"

"I'm fine." I took a large gulp of fresh air and started to walk again.

"Hey, Liv. Hey, Alice." Aiden smiled and gave us both a quick wave before continuing to stretch.

"Hi," I said breathlessly.

"Hey, nerd brain," Liv shouted at him and then started laughing as he shook his head. I could tell from his expression that he was surprised to see us there.

"Grow up, Liv." Aiden shook his head and he looked as if he wanted to say something else, but he didn't. Instead he looked at me and gave me a small smile before speaking. "Hey, Alice."

"Hey," I responded back with a small smile, my heart racing. I wanted to say more than "Hey." I wanted to say something witty and funny. I wanted to make him laugh and think to himself, "Wow, that Alice is funny, beautiful and smart. I need to get with her now!" Of course, me being me, all I said was "hey."

"So you two are interested in football now?" He raised an eyebrow at us as he continued stretching. "Or are you interested in the guys?"

"Very funny, Aiden," Liv said in a high tone. "My boyfriend had better not hear you say that."

"Hear him say what?" Xander suddenly appeared out of nowhere, and I watched as he looked Liv over appreciatively, as if he wanted to eat her up. I wished that Aiden would look at me the same way.

"Aiden was saying we're here to meet guys," Liv said in a decidedly snarky voice and I wanted to groan. Because what Aiden had said was partly true, only it was just me to meet men. And the man I was interested in getting to know better was him.

"Are you?" Xander grinned at her. "Because that would be awkward if you wanted to meet a guy here. What with me being here and all."

"Oh, really?" Liv said with her hands on her hips. "That's it? It would be awkward? That's all you have to say?"

"You don't think it would be awkward?"

"So you would be cool with me trying to hook up with another guy?" She sounded pissed, and I wanted to shake her. "You'd be fine, but slightly awkward?"

"Obviously not." Xander sighed. "Would it make you feel better if I said I would punch the guy in the face?"

"I don't believe in violence," Liv said with a straight face and then she giggled. "But yes, that makes me feel better."

"Hey, Liv!" Henry shouted as he ran onto the field. Henry was Xander's younger brother and he was divine looking. He had the same short dark hair and green eyes as Xander, and he was built like a soccer player, with long lean legs, muscular thighs and calves and a torso that looked like it had been carved by Michelangelo. "Hey, Alice." He grinned at me and whistled. "You two are looking mighty fine for a game of flag football."

"Thank you." I grinned at him as Liv laughed. I could see Xander and Aiden frowning as Henry walked up to us both and gave us a quick hug.

"I didn't know you girls were into football," he said as he stepped back.

"Well, you know." I shrugged, wanting to make sure Liv didn't say something stupid. "We wanted to get our exercising on."

"Yeah, we want washboard stomachs," Liv continued. "And perky asses."

"I wouldn't be complaining if either of you were my woman." Henry winked at us, and we both giggled.

"You know, Alice is single," Liv said and my face went beet red as Henry looked at me with an interested eye. "You guys should go out some time."

"I would like that." He nodded as he looked me up and down. "I would like that a lot."

"Shall we get started with the game?" Aiden's voice interrupted the moment and his eyes were shooting daggers at me as I looked over at him. "This is a field for flag football, not the local meet-up site for Match.com."

"Don't be a jerk." Liv shook her head at her brother and then looked at me and winked. "If Henry and Alice want to make plans to go on a hot date, then let them."

"Liv, seriously, grow up." Aiden's voice was stiff and he turned around and blew a whistle. "Hey, guys, we're about to get started." He shouted out to all the other people in the field. "Please gather around so we can pick teams."

"Bossy-boots as usual," Liv whispered to me as we walked to stand in the crowd of people in front of Aiden. "I swear I don't know why you want to date him. He's just way too annoying and obnoxious."

"Maybe that bossiness will be good in the bedroom," I whispered back to her. "Maybe it won't be as annoying."

"You'll have to let me know." She giggled. "Well, not any specific details, just if the sex makes up for it all."

"If we even get to have sex." I sighed. "At the rate this is going, it'll be a while."

"What will be a while?" Xander asked me as he stood next to us.

"Her and Aiden hooking up in the bedroom," Liv answered.

"I thought you guys have already hooked up?" He looked confused.

"Yeah, we had sex *once*," I said. "But I'm wondering if we will have sex again." For some reason, my voice grew louder and as I spoke, I realized that the field was silent and there were a few people looking at me.

"Are you ready, Alice?" Aiden said sarcastically as he stared at me. "Or would you like us to wait while you discuss your sex life?"

"Please go ahead," I squeaked out and glared at him. *Insufferable pig.* I looked away from him, angry that I had somehow turned back to my teenage self around him. I was older now. More confident. More capable. I wasn't some immature little teenager anymore. I was an adult, and I wasn't going to allow Aiden to make me feel like some naughty little kid. At least, not outside of the bedroom.

"I'M GLAD YOU'RE ON MY team." Henry smiled at me as we stood at the end of the field, panting.

"Me too." I smiled and took a deep breath. My heart was racing from all the running, and I just wanted to collapse onto the ground.

"The other team seems to be way too serious." He laughed and we watched as Aiden and Xander kept throwing the ball back and forth.

"I don't know how Aiden and Xander wound up on the same team." I laughed. "It almost seems unfair. Though I'm glad because that means I'm not paired with either of them."

"Poor Liv." Henry grinned and we watched as she kept yelling at the two men to pass her the ball.

"I know." I laughed. "Do you think we should run down there and try and grab the flags?"

"Nah, not yet." He shook his head. "Our teammates can handle the defense for now. Seems like you still need to catch your breath."

"Yeah." I nodded, not feeling embarrassed that he'd noticed what bad shape I was in. "I guess that's what I get for working in an office."

"What do you do?" he asked curiously.

"Nothing fun." I laughed. "I'm an assistant, secretary, receptionist for a real estate company." I made a face. "It's boring, but it pays the bills until I can do what I want to do."

"What do you want to do?"

"I'd love to be an actress." I smiled at him. "Isn't that what everyone says that works as an assistant?"

"No, I think that's what baristas normally say."

"True," I agreed and sighed. "Okay, that was a bit of a lie. I don't really want to be an actress."

"Oh?" He looked confused. "That's a weird lie."

"I know." I shook my head. "I'm an idiot. It just sounded more glorious than what I really want to do."

"What's that, then?" He scratched his forehead. "Let me guess."

"Okay, then, guess." I smiled.

"You want to be a preservationist and preserve insects?"

"Eww, no." I giggled.

"Okay, let me guess again." He pursed his lips and looked thoughtful, his green eyes alive with humor as he gazed at me. "You want to model lingerie at Victoria's Secret?"

"No!" I said emphatically, and he laughed.

"A man can hope." He winked at me and I could feel myself blushing. Was he flirting with me?

"That's never going to happen. That would be my worst nightmare."

"What would be your worst nightmare?" Liv came running towards me, her face a deep red and her eyes looking crazy and wild from all the exercise.

"Me being a lingerie model."

"What?" She stopped dead in her tracks and started laughing. "Who's gone and offered you that job, then?"

"No one offered me that job." I shook my head and rolled my eyes. "Henry was just saying that—"

"Liv!" Aiden ran up to us and shouted at his sister. "Stop bloody talking." He glared at her and blew his whistle. "Everyone stop!"

"What's up with the whistle?" Liv looked confused as all the players came to a halt. "What's going on?"

"That's what I want to know." Aiden frowned and gazed at me for a second before looking away. "Alice and Henry aren't doing anything, and now you're just standing there talking as well. Are you guys sure you want to be a part of these games?"

"I was playing!" Liv shouted. "I just stopped because Alice was telling me about her offer to be a lingerie model."

"I didn't say I was offered that job." I groaned.

"I think there has been some confusion," Henry spoke up. "Alice hasn't been offered that as a job yet, it's just her dream job to be a lingerie model at Victoria's Secret."

"No, it's not!" I screeched and looked at Aiden beseechingly. "Henry asked me if I wanted to model lingerie, and I said no."

"I don't care what the two of you talk about." Aiden's eyes narrowed as he gazed at me and shook his head. "Save your personal talk for after the game is done."

"I ... ugh." I closed my mouth in frustration. "I am playing. I was just trying to catch my breath because I was feeling a little tired from all the running back and forth."

"Maybe you can take her to your gym and help her work out," Liv suggested. "What do you say, Aiden?"

"I guess." He frowned, and my heart thudded at the thought of some one-on-one time with Aiden.

"You can come to my gym if you want." Henry grinned at me. "I make a great personal trainer."

"Oh, thanks." I looked at him with wide eyes. This wasn't part of the plan. I'd thought that Henry was just being nice to me, but now I wasn't so sure. Was he flirting with me for real?

"I think it would be fun." He winked at me. "Plus, then we can finish this conversation without having a whistle blown at us."

"Finish what conversation?" Aiden's eyes narrowed and he took a step towards us.

"Alice was telling me what she wants to be when she grows up." Henry smiled, seemingly unaware of the fact that Aiden wasn't looking very happy.

"She wants to be a casting agent for reality show TV stars." Aiden glanced at me as he spoke. "Though it kills me to call anyone who goes on a reality TV show a star."

"How did you know that?" I asked him in surprise.

"How could I not know that?" He shrugged. "You've mentioned it a billion times."

"I didn't know you ever bothered listening to me," I said softly.

"I always listen to you, Alice," he said, his eyes boring into mine intensely. However, I couldn't figure out what his gaze was telling me. Did he listen to me because he liked me or because I just talked too much?

"So that's why you said actress?" Henry put his arm around my shoulder, and I wanted to groan as Aiden pursed his lips and took a step back. I could see Liv's eyes gleaming at me with joy and excitement. She seemed to be the only one loving this little chat.

"Yeah, actress seemed a more dignified answer than casting for *The Bachelor*." I smiled at him, my face reddening as he rubbed the top of my shoulders innocently. Or at least, I thought he was rubbing them innocently.

"I don't know." He laughed. "Both seem to be pretty naughty professions."

"Naughty?" I looked at him with a curious expression. "Why naughty?"

"Are you two ready to play?" Xander interrupted this time, his green eyes looking at me with disapproval.

"I've been ready," I said in reply. "It wasn't me who stopped the game, it was Aiden."

"Yeah, Xander. It was Aiden who blew his whistle, like some sort of trumped-up referee." Liv glared at Xander. "This is just meant to be a friendly game. This isn't the NFL."

"They don't play flag football in the NFL," Xander replied to her with an amused smile.

"Exactly," she said with an annoyed expression. "This isn't the NFL."

"Liv, if you and Alice don't want to play flag football, then you can both just leave." Aiden spoke up this time and my heart stopped. "When we're playing the game, we should be playing the game. We aren't here to hear about your sex lives or the sexy lingerie you're buying. Or how much you need to work out because you can't keep up with the rest of us."

I gasped at his words and my mouth fell open. My face was hot with humiliation, and I glared at his smug and superior expression. Was he calling me a fat ass?

"Aiden, you're such a pompous jerk." Liv just shook her head and then looked at Xander. "And you're an asshole."

"I'm an asshole?" He put his hands up in the air. "I didn't even say anything."

"Exactly. How could you let Aiden speak to us like that?"

"What?" Xander sounded frustrated. I was about to cut in and say something when Henry cleared his throat loudly.

"Look, guys, this is my fault," he said smoothly. "I was the one talking to Alice and monopolizing her time. I won't do it on the field anymore. I'll just wait until we go out for drinks later."

"Whatever," Aiden said and then blew his whistle again. "If everyone is ready to begin playing again, maybe we can get back to the game."

"We were playing the game before you stopped us, Aiden," Liv said loudly. "I think we're all ready to get back to something other than you trying to boss us around."

"Grow up, Liv." Aiden rolled his eyes. "I thought you'd start acting your age now that you have a boyfriend."

"Excuse me?" Liv walked over to him, and I watched as Xander grabbed her around the waist and pulled her towards him and whispered something in her ear. She turned to me then and gave me an exasperated look as if to say, "Why do you want to date my brother again? He's a big old jerk."

And then, because the day was going so perfectly already, my luck got even better. "I'm here, folks!" A loud boyish voice echoed across the field, and we all turned to watch as Scott came running towards us, a huge grin on his handsome face. My stomach flipped anxiously as he ran directly towards me. This was the last thing that I needed. I was supposed to be making Aiden jealous and antsy with random guys, not his sister's boyfriend's rich brother or his own brother. I could still remember the night that Aiden had spotted Scott kissing me, and I wanted to scream out in frustration. Why was this happening to me? Why was it that the guys I didn't want paying attention to me were circling around me like vultures?

"Hey, Alice." Scott stopped right next to me and gave me a kiss on the cheek. "Fancy seeing you here."

"Hey," I said weakly, and I gazed at Aiden quickly. He was staring at me with a closed expression on his face, and I offered him a small smile, which he didn't return.

"I heard you were going to be playing so I—"

"Eeeep!" Aiden blew his whistle loudly and interrupted Scott. "Scott, you can be on Alice's team. And you guys can talk later. At the bar." He looked at me then and smirked slightly. "Just remember to take a number, though, as Henry's already got his ticket ready to talk to her first." And with that he blew his whistle again and turned around. I could tell that everyone on the field, except for Liv, Xander and I, was confused about what was going on. All I could think about was getting back at Aiden for being such a prickhead. I was going to pay once I got him into my bed, of course. I thought back to what Xander had said about Aiden being a Dom, and I knew then exactly what I was going to try and do. I was going to make Aiden think I wanted to submit to him, but instead of letting him dominate me, I was going to tease him until he begged me to stop. Only then would I be able to wipe that smug little smirk from his way-too-handsome face.

"Next game, we need to kick their asses," Liv whispered in my ear as she glared at her brother.

"Yup," I said back to her. "Next game, we need to show them that we girls can kick ass at football as well."

SIX

The way to a man's lap
is through a horror movie

"ARGH, MY MUSCLES ARE STILL sore from football." I groaned as my calf muscles tingled. "Why am I in such bad shape?"

"So am I." Liv made a face. "We need to start working out."

"That doesn't sound like fun." I made a face at her.

"We'll go to the gym and walk on the treadmill," she said and nodded to herself. "And maybe we can practice throwing the football at the park."

"Why?"

"So we can practice," she said. "I want us to show up and just totally dominate the game. We need to show Aiden and Xander that we aren't just weak, unsporty girls. I totally didn't appreciate how they basically excluded me from every play."

"I know," I agreed. "That was so uncool."

"Yeah, we need to show those boys that girls can kick ass in sports as well."

"I guess so." I sighed and stretched my legs out. "Though I don't know I will ever kick ass in football."

"Yes, you will, Alice. You need to have a positive mental attitude."

"I'm trying," I said and sighed. "I mean, I'm still trying to have a positive attitude about Aiden and me getting together."

"About that ..." Liv said and grinned. "Let's go over the plan." She looked down at her notepad and then back up at me. "I'm going to invite Aiden over to watch a movie as a way for us to make up for the argument that went down." She made a face. "He thinks that we were inappropriate on the football field yesterday and that we shouldn't argue like that in front of others."

"Since when has he cared about being an ass in front of others?" I was surprised, but pleased to hear that he was going to be coming over.

"Since he realized I'm not a little kid anymore." She laughed. "Anyway, I'm going to tell him to bring a movie and a bottle of wine and that is how he can make it up to me."

"But you're not going to be here, right?" I said, trying to confirm that the plan was the same as this morning.

"Yeah, well, I'll be here when he arrives, but just before the movie starts, I'm going to leave abruptly because Xander is going to need me."

"He knows he's going to need you, right?" I asked skeptically; I wasn't sure we could count on Xander following through in helping us with our plan.

"Trust me, he knows he's going to need me." She grinned. "I told him to call me at eight p.m. on the dot. I'll talk to him and then leave and then you and Aiden can watch the movie. I told Aiden to get a horror movie—"

"Oh no, you know I hate horror movies." I groaned.

"That's why I told him to bring one. You'll scream and jump into his arms, and he'll protect you."

"Protect me from the TV?"

"Well, he'll put his arm around you to comfort you from the scariness on the screen or whatever, and you can snuggle into his arms." Liv sounded impatient. "Come on, Alice, you know how it goes. You're the one who taught me the horror-movie trick."

"I know." I sighed. "I just don't think it will work on Aiden."

"It works on all men." Liv grinned. "Even guys who are totally into themselves and have significant others; though it's unlikely to lead to kissing and messing around with them."

"It's unlikely to lead to kissing for me and Aiden, either."

"Alice," Liv sighed. "Just go with it, please."

"Fine." I shrugged. "I'll watch a horror movie with him, but I just hope he doesn't feel like he was tricked and leave. He didn't exactly seem like he was into me at the football game."

"We were running up and down a field, he didn't have time to flirt."

"I guess so." I laughed. "Let's be real, Liv. What he was doing was the opposite of flirting."

"He was just being a typical macho jealous guy." Liv rolled her eyes. "Trust me, he's into you. Even Xander thinks he's into you. Though he still hasn't told me that he told you that Aiden was a Dom." She looked annoyed. "And I hinted around it as well."

"Oh, Alice." I shook my head. "You're not meant to know, remember?" I played with my hair for a few seconds and then continued talking. "And Xander really does think Aiden's into me?" I asked hopefully.

"Yes." She grinned. "Though he also thinks Scott and Henry are into you, too. Oh and that other guy as well, what's-his-face."

"Who is what's-his-face?"

"Jackson. The one guy who kept trying to tackle you."

"Oh, the tall guy with the crooked nose and bleach-blond hair?" I made a face. "I swear he was trying to grab my tits."

"Yup, him." Liv laughed. "He tried to do that to me, too, and Xander elbowed him."

"Oh, Xander!" I laughed.

"Yeah." She giggled. "I love it when he acts all jealous. Anyway, back to what I was going to say. This is the perfect opportunity for you to mention that you've always been interested in experimenting."

"Experimenting?" I frowned. "With what? Drugs?"

"No, silly." Liv laughed and shook her head. "Experimenting in the bedroom."

"Oh." My face went red. "You think I should tell him I want to know what it's like to be a sub?" I bit my lower lip. "Isn't it too soon for me to be bringing that up?"

"Yes, it's too soon. No way should you mention anything about wanting to be a sub." She shuddered and made a face. "That's way too obvious and honestly, I don't want to think of you and my brother in a Dom and sub relationship." Her voice grew as melodramatic as it had the morning after game night when I'd told her what Xander had told me.

"So what should I say?"

"Just say something like, you've always been intrigued by couples in alternative lifestyles and you wish you could meet a man who could possess and dominate you."

"I'm not saying that." I gave her a look and laughed. "In fact, there is no way in hell I'm saying anything close to that. That's just as bad as me talking about being a sub and him being a Dom."

"I think it sounds good," Liv said with a sigh. "But fine, maybe say, I wish I could meet a man that likes to take charge."

"Eh." I groaned. "That just sounds like I'm asking him to take me to the bedroom."

"Don't you want him to do that?" She winked at me.

"No, I do not want him to take me to the bed after I've made a comment like that. That would just be because he thinks I'm begging for him to jump my bones."

"Aren't you?"

"Well, yes." I laughed. "But I don't want him to jump my bones because he thinks I'm some sort of sex fiend, begging to be taken and dominated by him."

"He's not going to think that," Liv said. "Trust me."

"Yeah, well, I'm not saying that. I'll think of something."

"Wear something sexy as well."

"Liv, how am I going to wear something sexy? It's not like I can wear some sexy teddy, since you're going to be there as well." I shook my head. "Liv, come on now."

"I know, I know. I just want you guys to get together so badly." She rubbed her hands together excitedly. "Could you imagine? We can go on double dates and on trips together."

"That would be cool," I agreed. "What does Xander think of all of this?"

"I don't know." She made a face. "I'm still upset that he told you not to tell me that Aiden is a Dom."

"He's just trying to protect you."

"I guess, but I mean, come on, why can't I know that my brother is a Dom?"

"Please don't tell Xander I told you." I was worried that Liv would tell Xander, and then Xander would be mad at me and then he wouldn't provide me with any new information about Aiden. And I needed new information on Aiden as much as a coke addict needed coke, maybe even more than that. And I knew that Liv wasn't going to be the provider of any real and useful information about her brother.

"I won't." She made a face. "Now back to your outfit—what are you going to wear?"

"I don't know." I shook my head. "I don't want to be too obvious. Especially because he has a girlfriend."

"He doesn't have a girlfriend. He just went on a few dates with that girl."

"He went on a few dates?" I said quickly. "How do you know?"

"Well, I only know about the one," Liv responded. "But I assume they went out more than once, right?"

"I guess." I groaned. "Why does that ho have to be after my man?" I looked at Liv's giggling face and groaned again. "I'm horrible, aren't I? I bet she's a great girl and here I am calling her a ho. She's nothing like a ho."

"Oh?"

"She went to Dartmouth for undergrad," I said quickly. "And she has a pet dog and a hamster and she enjoys playing racquetball."

"Huh?" Liv's eyes widened. "How do you know all that?"

"Google is my friend." I laughed. "Plus, she has a blog where she talks about her life." I rolled my eyes. "And she has photos of Frodo, her hamster, and Blackie, her dog."

"Please don't tell me her dog is black."

"He is." I nodded and giggled. "Who calls their black dog Blackie?"

"So unoriginal," Liv agreed. "She has to go. You're much better for Aiden."

"Yeah, right. I doubt he thinks so."

"He's an idiot," she said and pulled out her phone as it beeped. "Okay, that was Aiden, he'll be here at seven-ish."

"Oh my God. What am I going to wear?" I squealed. "And does he know I'll be here?"

"Of course he knows," Liv said. "Where else would you be?"

"Yeah," I said weakly. "Where else would I be?"

I WAITED AT THE COFFEE shop two blocks away from our apartment for Liv to text me to let me know that Aiden had arrived. We'd decided that I wouldn't be at the apartment when he arrived. Instead, I'd arrive back home about thirty minutes after he arrived and talk about my hot date.

I have to admit I felt like a bit of a tart, sitting in the coffee shop in my short black mini-skirt and short white top, with my red push-up bra and high heels. I could see an old man in the corner of the store staring at me, his eyes moving up and down my body as if I were a fine piece of art that was to be looked over microscopically so that he didn't miss any tiny details.

I sipped on my now-cold latte and stared at the screen on my phone, hoping that Liv would just hurry up and text me. Already I was regretting the lies I was going to be telling Aiden when I arrived back home. I wasn't even sure he'd believe me. I mean, who goes for a date in a black mini skirt and arrives back home at 7:30 p.m.? I knew that when I arrived back home, he was either going to think I was a whore or a liar, and I wasn't exactly pleased with either of those options.

"Good evening, ma'am." A deep voice sounded next to me, and I looked up to see the old man standing beside me. I tried not to cringe as I smelled him and looked into his wrinkly face. He looked even older than I'd thought before. He was in his late sixties and had scraggly grey hair and a missing tooth.

"Hello," I said lightly, my voice coming out as a squeak.

"How much, then?" He sat down in the chair across from me and winked.

"Sorry?" I frowned and turned my face slightly to the right. He really did smell bad, like rotten eggs.

"How much?" he said again and pulled out a twenty dollar bill. "What does twenty get me?"

"What does twenty get you?" I repeated dumbly. Yes, I just might be the dumbest and most immature twenty-two-year-old in the world.

"A blowjob or some titty action as well?" His voice lowered and I gasped.

"What?" I stood up, feeling enraged. "Who the hell do you think you're talking to?"

"Uhm?" He looked around with a somewhat frightened face, which I thought was ironic. Wasn't I the one who should look frightened? He was the one coming up to me and acting as if I were a prostitute.

"Get out of here, you dirty old man!" I said more loudly, and I could see a young couple in the corner looking at us with big eyes and awkward smiles. Ugh! I was so annoyed that I grabbed my coffee and left the store. I was mad at myself for having gone along with Liv's idea. It was stupid and I didn't even think that Aiden would care if he thought I'd been on a date. On what sort of date would I be going out looking like a hooker, but making it home before 8 p.m.? Only a lame date, and what was there to be jealous of if the date sucked?

I got into my car and drove home feeling bummed. I turned on the radio and smiled as I heard "I'm Not the Only One" playing. I sang along with Sam Smith and tried to keep my mind off of how much my life was sucking. I wasn't sure why I was so bad in relationships. I wasn't sure why I couldn't approach Aiden and just be normal. I wasn't sure why I couldn't just flirt and be honest. I think it had to do with my childhood, which seemed to be everyone's story.

My father had left my mother and me when I was two. I couldn't really even remember him, if I was honest. My mother had remarried when I was four and my stepfather had adopted me. He even treated me as if I were his kid, and I loved him and called him dad. However, I always wondered about my real dad. I hadn't seen him since I was two. When he'd left, he'd never looked back. It hadn't really hit me until I was fifteen. When I was fifteen, I decided I wanted to find him, so I looked him up online and was able to locate him. I'd called him and found out that he had a new family and two more children. He'd said he was going to call me back and we would go to dinner. He never called, but I didn't give up. I called him back and he said he'd have me over for Sunday lunch to meet the family. He'd said to call him back in a few days to get the address. I'd called and the number had been disconnected and I'd never heard from him again. I hadn't tried to make contact with him again either. I knew that deep inside of me there was pain that emanated from my father's rejection, but I tried not to dwell on it. Instead, I tried to look at the bright side of life, the fun side of life. I tried to be goofy and to laugh and to just ignore the things that made me feel bad. However, now it wasn't so easy.

My heart felt heavy as I pulled into a parking space and turned the ignition off. I think that being in a situation where you think you love someone and they don't love you is most probably one of the hardest things in life. While I still had hope (for what are we without hope?), I didn't necessarily think I had a good shot, no matter how much Liv tried to convince us both otherwise. Part of me felt like a fool with all the plans and tricks. I didn't think they would work on Aiden. Not given our history. I didn't think they would work, but that didn't mean I wasn't still going to try. Aiden had been a part of my heart since I could remember. He most probably didn't even know how much he meant to me. He most probably didn't realize that he was the reason why my heart had healed after my father's rejection.

"I'M BACK FROM MY DATE," I squealed as I opened the door to the apartment, with a wide fake smile on my face. "He got me roses," I called out giddily. If I was going to lie, I might as well play it up. Silence met my lies, and I frowned as I hurried through the corridor to the living room. "Liv?" I said in a confused voice, surprised that she wasn't responding as planned. "Liv," I said again as I entered the living room.

"She's gone out," Aiden said smoothly with a short smile from the couch. He was sitting there stiffly with an amused look on his face. "She asked me to wait as she had tried to call and text you, but you weren't picking up."

"Oh?" I frowned and looked at my phone. "I don't have any missed calls." I made a face and checked the screen again.

"I was there as she called you." He shrugged and I sighed.

"I bet my service went out again." I shook my head. "I'm going to change carriers, I'm so fed up of this crap. I'm always missing calls."

"I thought maybe you were just ignoring her because of your hot date," he said as he glanced at me curiously. My face was red with shame as I looked away from him. "So where are they, then?"

"Where are what?" I frowned as I looked back at him.

"The roses?"

"The roses?" I repeated dumbly, but I knew exactly what he was talking about. Me and my big mouth had remembered to pretend my date had given me flowers, but I'd forgotten to buy them at the grocery store on the way home.

"That your date gave you. What was his name again?"

"His name?" I squeaked.

"Yes, his name." Aiden frowned. "Or you don't want to tell me?"

"I, uh ..." I swallowed hard, my mind going blank.

"Were you out with Scott?"

"Scott?" I made a face. "No, of course not."

"Henry?"

"Henry, Xander's brother?" I asked in surprise.

"Yes, the one and only. The guy you were flirting with all day at flag football."

"I was not flirting with him." I rolled my eyes and made a face at him.

"Don't tell me you plan to slip into his bed as well."

"How rude!" My jaw dropped. "I can't believe that you would say that." I peered into his azure blue eyes, and I could see remorse in his gaze.

"That was a low blow," he said finally. "Sorry."

"Yeah." I stood there awkwardly. This was not going as planned at all. "Why are you still here?" I said curiously. "Liv is gone."

"She figured we could still watch the movie together when you got in."

"But you didn't know when I'd be back."

"I was willing to wait," he said simply, and my stomach started flittering.

"Oh?" My heart jumped.

"Yeah, I wanted to watch this movie, and Elizabeth doesn't do horror movies."

"Oh," I said and this time my heart dropped.

"I thought Liv and I would watch it, but you'll do as well."

"Oh, wow, how flattering." I rolled my eyes. "I'll do, huh?"

"Yeah, you'll do." He laughed. "You going to sit or do you want to change first?"

"Change?" I raised an eyebrow at him as I caught him checking out my long expanse of leg.

"Yeah, change." He raised an eyebrow back at me. "I'm not sure I'll be able to keep my hands to myself otherwise."

"Oh." I blushed, but all I was thinking inside was, *You don't need to keep your hands to yourself.*

"That's an interesting outfit that you're wearing to a first date." He looked up to my heaving bosom. "A bit revealing, don't you think?"

"Yeah, maybe you're right," I said with a grin. "I had a guy ask me if I was a prostitute."

"What?" He laughed.

"Well, he asked me what twenty dollars would get him."

"Oh no!" He laughed again and then paused. "This wasn't your date, was it?"

"Technically yes, it was the guy I met tonight," I said and burst out laughing. It was true. The guy in the coffee shop was the only guy I had met tonight. He was as close to a date as I'd come.

"Oh, I'm sorry." He bit his lower lip to stop from laughing even more. "So maybe it wasn't really a perfect date?"

"Yeah, it wasn't a perfect date." I sighed. "And there were no roses. I was just saying that so Liv wouldn't feel bad for me." I felt bad about lying, but I didn't want him to know that I knew Liv wasn't going to be there.

"I kinda figured that part out." He grinned. "Go and change and let's watch this movie and maybe we can change this night around."

"Can we order pizza as well?" I asked hopefully, as my stomach grumbled.

"I think that can be arranged." He nodded.

"Yay!" I felt like I was soaring as I stared at Aiden. This was going better than planned, and I had kinda extricated myself from my lie about my date. I knew I hadn't come completely clean, but I figured I had admitted enough. "Pepperoni and—"

"Pepperoni and ham with onions," he said, interrupting me and giving me a wink. "I know, Alice, trust me, I know."

"I wasn't sure if you'd remember," I said with a shrug, though of course I was deliriously happy inside.

"You and Liv ordered pizza almost every weekend." He rolled his eyes. "And you were both brats about not letting me choose what went on half of the pizza, so of course I remember."

"Are you calling me a brat?" I asked, with my hand on my hip.

"What do you think?" he asked with a grin.

"I think you're calling me a brat." I wrinkled my nose at him and took a step forward.

"You got smarter in your old age." He laughed and my eyes narrowed.

"I'm going to make you pay for that." I took another step forward and raised my fists at him.

"Is this your way of trying to touch me, old lady?" He raised an eyebrow and I gasped. How had he known that I was hoping to cop a quick feel? Could he see from my expression that I was practically salivating at how sexy he looked?

"Haha, very funny. I'm not an old lady, and I don't care about touching you."

"Is that right?" He grabbed my arms and pulled me towards him. "That's a pity."

"What's a pity?"

"That you don't care about touching me," he said lightly as his hands ran down my arm.

"Oh, why?" I breathed out, my heart about to jump out of my chest.

"Because I very much like being touched." He winked and then stepped back. "Now go and change, and I'll order the pizza. We don't want to be up all night."

"I don't mind," I whispered under my breath as I hurried out of the room. And I didn't mind. Not at all. He could keep me up for twenty-four hours straight if he wanted to. Shit, thirty-six hours if he begged. I could picture him now, kissing my neck and pleading with me to stay awake so that he could have me one more time. How delicious would it feel to have his body against mine, on top of me, sliding himself inside of me? It would feel like heaven.

"Alice?"

"Uh, yes." I looked around, my face bright red.

"You okay? You were walking and then just stopped."

"Oh, I'm fine." I nodded. "Thanks." I gulped and hurried out of the room to my bedroom. I needed to stop fantasizing about being with Aiden. I needed for us to either get together or not. I was acting like a fool because all I could think about was the sexual tension between us. I opened my closet and pulled out some tank tops and T-shirts. I didn't know what to wear. I didn't want to wear my Mickey Mouse T-shirt as that was too childish and unsexy, but I also didn't want to wear a tight tank top and make him think that I was trying to turn him on. I also wasn't sure whether to go braless or not. If it was just Liv and me, I wouldn't have thought about it twice. My bra would have been off in seconds, but then I also wouldn't have thought twice about putting on a T-shirt with cartoon characters on it when I was with Liv. I finally settled on a black wife-beater with a pushup bra (your breasts can never look too high and luscious) and a pair of black boy-shorts. Hey—I have long legs; I have to show them off. I did have to make a quick trip to the bathroom to give myself a quick dry shave because I could see the beginnings of hair stubble on my legs and I didn't want Aiden running his hands over my calves and thinking he was touching bristle or something.

"Hey," I said casually as I sauntered back into the living room and frowned as he said "Hey" back without even looking up at me. I'd just spent fifteen minutes applying makeup in order to look subtly beautiful and he wasn't even going to look at me? Grr!

"Did you order the pizza?" I asked, standing in front of him.

"Yup," he said as he played with his phone. I could feel my face growing hot as I stood there, feeling like a fool.

"Cool," I said, not knowing what else to say. It's not like I could say, *Hey, Aiden, look at me. I look pretty right now and I want you to take in my hot body as I stand in the pose that I know elongates my neck and makes my stomach look flat.* Of course I didn't say that. I just stood there for a few more seconds before plopping down on the couch next to him and sitting back.

"Ready for the movie?" Aiden finally glanced at me before turning the TV on. He didn't even look at me for five seconds. I was positive he hadn't even noticed how blue my eyes looked with my new Lancome mascara.

"Sure," I said snappily.

"Uh oh?" he said and I felt his eyes on me again. "What is it, Alice?"

"What is what?" I looked up at him and there was a sparkle in his eyes as he looked at me.

"Why are you so grouchy?"

"Who said I'm grouchy?" I glared at him. Stupid Aiden with his stupid smirk and pink lips making me feel like a petulant child.

"Smile, Alice." He leaned over and started to tickle me.

"Stop it." I laughed and pushed him away.

"But I want to see the smile on your face." He grinned and continued to tickle me under my arms and on my knees.

"Aiden," I squeaked out. "Stop!" I laughed and tried to push him away.

"I see you're still as ticklish as you were before." He grinned as I laughed and I grabbed his hands.

"Aiden," I breathed out, my face dangerously close to his.

"Yes, Alice?" he said lightly and moved even closer to me.

"Stop," I said as I fell against him. "Please."

"You didn't say that the last time I tickled you," he said with a devilish look in his eyes. "In fact, you quite liked it then." He moved towards my ear. I felt his lips next to my earlobe and he blew into it lightly.

"Aiden!" I screamed and jumped off of the couch, my heart racing as memories came flashing back. The last time Aiden had tickled me had been the night we'd spent together. He had been inside of me, not moving, and I'd wondered what was going on. Then he'd moved his lips to my ear and he'd sucked on my earlobe and then I'd felt his tongue and breath in my ear. And I'd giggled because it had tickled me. I'd squirmed underneath him and then he'd started moving inside of me again, all the while continuing to breathe into my ear. It had been the most amazing and surreal experience of my life. Every nerve-ending in my body had been on edge, and when I'd exploded in orgasm every part of my body felt the pleasure. At the time, I'd known it had been a breathtaking experience, but it was only now that I'd been with other men that I knew that it was a one-of-a-kind experience. No man had ever pleasured me as much as Aiden had that night.

"Sorry." He grinned. "I was just teasing you. I won't tickle you again."

"What were you talking about when you said that I didn't say that the last time you tickled me?" I asked him as I sat back on the couch. I curled my legs up under me and looked at him curiously. Okay, so I was acting. I was pretty sure I knew what he was talking about. I mean, that was a moment I'd never forget. However, I wanted him to tell me what he thought about that night. I wanted him to tell me that he still remembered what it was like to be with me.

"You know what moment I'm talking about, Alice." He stared at my lips and then back up to my eyes. "So is there a reason why you're asking me?"

"No," I said and looked down. *Busted!*

"Shall we start the movie and pause it when the pizza arrives?" he asked, and I was slightly annoyed that he was changing the subject. When was he going to just let us talk about that night and let us discuss everything without changing the subject?

"That's fine," I said because I didn't want to start the night off trying to get all serious with him. I knew that there was some sort of attraction between us, but I wasn't sure exactly what it was and what he really thought about me. Especially now that he was dating Elizabeth Jeffries.

THE PIZZA ARRIVED FIFTEEN MINUTES after we'd started the movie and I was happy for the break. The movie was called *Orphan*, and it was already creeping me out. Unfortunately, I didn't feel like Aiden and I were in the "let me jump into your lap and bury my face in your shoulder" stage yet, so I just had to sit through it and try to not close my eyes.

"Ready to start the movie again?" he asked me softly and I nodded, my mouth full of pizza. Aiden stood up and turned the lights off and then came back to the couch to press play.

"In the dark?" I mumbled, my mouth full of delicious greasy pizza.

"We can't watch a scary movie and not be in the dark." He grinned and pressed play. I stifled a groan and watched as the weird-looking kid with big eyes came back onto the screen. I knew she was evil. There was no way she wasn't going to be evil. Why couldn't her new parents see that? My heart thudded as I waited for something to happen. I became so engrossed in the movie that I didn't even realize that Aiden was shifting closer and closer to me on the couch or that his arm was around my shoulders, or that I was leaning back into him. I didn't realize until there was a really scary scene and I screamed and I found my head against his chest. His chest felt hard and warm and he smelled so good and musky, like sandalwood and sand on a balmy night by the ocean. I breathed him in and tried not to kiss his chest. I wanted to consume him and his scent.

"You okay?" His voice was amused, and I felt his hands rubbing my back and massaging my shoulders.

"This movie is scary," I said softly. I wondered if he could feel my heart racing.

"It is a horror movie." He chuckled close to my ear, and I felt my body growing warm as he shifted on the couch.

"I know it's a horror movie." I moved back slightly, but his hands held me to him. "That doesn't mean I don't still get scared."

"Don't worry, Alice." His fingers played with my hair. "I'll take care of you."

"You think I'm a baby," I said and looked into his eyes.

"I don't think you're a baby," he said and moved his face closer to mine.

"You don't?" I said and moved even closer to him.

"No," he said. "If I did, I wouldn't be doing this, would I?" And he pressed his lips against mine.

"Hmm," I said and closed my eyes. I grabbed the back of his head and brought him closer to me. I felt his fingers in my hair as well and a part of me melted. His lips were gentle and firm next to mine, and I felt his tongue sliding into my mouth roughly as his kiss became deeper and more assertive. His fingers ran down my back, and I pressed myself into him, allowing my breasts to graze his muscular chest.

He groaned as I shifted on his lap and I reveled in the guttural sound. It was manly, strong and lusty, and it made me feel powerful. I shifted in his lap again and his fingers tightened on my waist and shifted me farther towards him.

"You taste like peaches," he muttered against my lips, and I sucked on his lower lip for a few seconds, tugging on it gently and then nibbling it with my teeth gently. "Oh, Alice." He groaned and ran his fingers down the side of my body, going slowly over the sides of my breasts.

"Yes, Aiden?"

"What are we doing?" He shook his head and his eyes gazed into mine questioningly.

"Whatever we want," I said softly as bells went off in my head. "I think we're both adults. We can do whatever we want to do." I ran my hands through his hair and kissed him again. I could feel a bulge underneath me and I knew that he was hard. I hid a smile and shifted on his lap again so that I could rub my ass on his hardness.

"Alice." He grabbed my waist again and held me still. "Didn't you have a date tonight?"

"Perhaps." I gave him a small smile. "But I'm not in a relationship. I'm still waiting for a guy that's as adventurous as me," I said, dropping the first crumb onto the ground for him to consume.

"Adventurous?" He looked at me curiously and I tried to hide my triumphant smile. I wanted to come straight out and tell him that I knew that he was interested in BDSM. I wanted to tell him I knew he was a Dom. I wanted to tell him that I was willing to try almost anything in the bedroom with him; that I'd had a crush on him for years and that part of me felt like I'd been falling in love with him for years as well, but I knew I couldn't tell him all that.

"Yes, I want a man who can take me on journeys I've never been on in the bedroom," I said simply and stared into his eyes with a small smile. "I want a man who can teach me things I didn't already know about."

"You want someone to teach you things?" he asked with a raised eyebrow.

"Yes." I nodded. "I want a professor. I'm willing to be his student," I said boldly, knowing that I was being very obvious.

"Have you found the guy?" he asked and I watched as he licked his lips. I felt as if he could hear my heart thudding as I stared at him.

"Perhaps," I said coyly.

"Perhaps, huh?" he said with a smirk. "You always were a sly one, Alice."

"I'm not sly." I shook my head.

"I think a twenty-two-year-old Aiden would beg to differ." He laughed.

"I wasn't thinking," I said with a blush. "I just wanted to be with you."

"I took your virginity," he said softly and I couldn't tell if he was asking a question or just stating a fact. I didn't answer him.

"But you knew it was me and you still went ahead."

"Yes, I did." He nodded.

"Why?" I held my breath.

"Why do you think?" He cocked his head and stared at me, seriously this time.

"I don't know." I bit my lower lip and then slowly got off of his lap. "Do you want to go to my room?" I asked him softly and reached down and grabbed his hand.

"Your room?"

"Yes, my bedroom." I gazed at him, not disguising the lust in my eyes. I fluffed my hair and stood there, basically offering myself on a platter. "I have handcuffs in my room."

"Handcuffs?" He repeated my words and stared at me for a few seconds taking in what I was offering. Then his phone started beeping. I saw him look at his phone and then frown slightly. He jumped up, placed his phone on the coffee table and looked at me. "Excuse me, I need to go to the restroom."

"Oh, okay," I said and watched as he left the room. And then I did something that I knew I shouldn't do. I'm not normally a nosey person—I swear I'm not—but I couldn't stop myself from looking at his phone. I pressed the screen with my fingers and to my astonishment the phone came to life. There was no lock on the screen, and I froze as I realized that I could just press the messages icon and see who had texted him. And of course, whose name did I see when I pressed messages? None other than Elizabeth Jeffries.

I groaned and made a face at the phone before turning to the doorway to make sure that Aiden wasn't on his way back in yet. I listened carefully and I could hear him humming in the bathroom. I smiled to myself and grabbed his phone, once again looking around the room, even though I knew I was the only one there. I clicked on Elizabeth's name, feeling guilty. My face was warm as my fingers fumbled on the screen. I looked around the room again and up at the ceiling, as if I thought that someone had placed hidden cameras in the room just to trap me in this moment. I heard a creak and dropped the phone as my heart thudded. Had Aiden snuck out of the bathroom without me noticing? Was I about to be busted before I'd even gotten to read the messages? I took a deep breath as I realized that the noise had come from my upstairs neighbors. I quickly grabbed the phone off of the floor and checked that it wasn't cracked. The last thing I wanted was to have to buy Aiden a brand new iPhone. My handbag fund was getting lower and lower each month.

I pressed home on the phone and quickly got back to the messages screen again. I clicked on Elizabeth Jeffries's name and waited for the messages to load. I looked at the smiley face at the bottom of the screen and frowned. How dare they send smiley faces to each other? I quickly scrolled up the screen so that I could read all the messages that were available on the phone before Aiden walked back into the room. I rolled my eyes at the obvious flirting. Elizabeth was asking him if he wanted to come over to try her lasagna. *Lasagna, my ass*, I thought as I read the message. Then she asked him over to try her roast chicken. Then they talked about going to the museum and she was thanking him for taking her. My fingers gripped the phone as I read a message from her asking him if he wanted to go camping this weekend. He'd responded with a flirty message saying "only if you promise to keep the bears away from me" and she'd replied, "Don't worry, I'll protect you." I could feel my face growing warm as I kept reading. My stomach was churning and my head was starting to pound. I was starting to feel upset. Why was Aiden flirting back with her if he liked me? How could he kiss me, but go to her house for frigging pasta? What was going on here? Did he like Elizabeth or did he like me? And was that why he'd gone to the bathroom as soon as he'd gotten her text? Had he gotten carried away with himself with me on his lap? And then her text had reminded him of her? I frowned as I put his phone back down on the desk. All of a sudden, I didn't feel so light and excited.

"Hey, sorry about that." Aiden walked back into the room with a smile and then looked at his watch.

"No worries," I said, trying not to stare at his lips. Lips I'd just been kissing. Lips I wanted to feel against mine once more.

"I should go," he said as he walked towards me. "I just realized the time."

"Oh," I said, my face growing red in embarrassment. He was going? Right after I'd asked him to come to my room and talked about wanting to experiment? I felt shame filling me as I realized he was blowing me off.

"Unless you want to finish watching the movie first and need someone to protect you?" He rubbed my shoulder and I offered him a weak smile.

"I'm fine," I said stiffly. How had we gone from making out to polite acquaintances in five minutes? I sighed inwardly as I realized that I just couldn't figure Aiden Taylor out.

"Okay, well, I'm sorry you had a bad date." He gave me a pointed look and paused, but I didn't say anything. "Thanks for a good night."

"Yeah, you're welcome," I said, not really sure how to respond. I mean, what did you say to a comment like that? Thanks for letting me sit on your lap and kiss you? Thanks for letting me feel your hardness on my ass as I sucked on your lip? Thanks for grazing my breasts and making me feel like I'm on fire? And the good kind of fire, not the scary "I might burn" fire, but the hot, sensuous, "I'm going to get laid and it's going to be amazing" fire.

"Have a good night, okay?" he said softly and I watched as he moved in closer to me. His eyes gazed into mine, and I held my breath as he gave me a light kiss on the lips. "See you later, Alice," he said as he pulled back, and all I could do was nod like an idiot as he picked up his phone and walked out of the room, leaving me in a daze. I had no idea what had just happened, but I knew that there was a distinct change in our relationship. I just didn't know what it meant.

SEVEN

Coffee dates aren't always dates

"COME ON, ALICE, AIDEN IS going to be meeting me at the coffee shop in about fifteen minutes, so you need to hurry." Liv poked her head into my bedroom and clapped her hands to rouse me.

"I just woke up." I stretched and groaned as I stared at Liv. "And I can't just show up by myself."

"Tell him that I told you to meet me there as well." She grinned. "And then I'll text and say I couldn't make it."

"Liv," I whined, not wanting to go but still jumping out of bed and opening my closet quickly to find something to wear. "I'm not going by myself," I said and looked at her. "He invited you to coffee, not me. And after last night, there is no way in hell that I'm putting myself out there again."

"Just hurry, Alice." She sighed, but she didn't try and change my mind. I had told Liv all about the previous evening when she'd gotten home and even she was wondering what Aiden was up to. "I tried to wake you up earlier and you didn't respond."

"I was sleeping," I groaned and pulled a T-shirt on over my tank top. "How do I look?" I glanced at Liv and she glanced back at me quickly.

"Great, now brush your teeth quickly. You don't want morning breath."

"Argh, I hate morning breath." I ran to the bathroom and grabbed my toothbrush and quickly filled it with a generous dollop of Aquafresh.

"And wash your face, too. You have booboo in your eyes."

"That's because I was sleeping just three minutes ago." I yawned dramatically.

"What do you care about more? Sleep or love?"

"At this moment, sleep," I groaned and yelped as I felt Liv brushing the knots out of my hair. "Liv!" I whimpered as I spat my toothpaste into the sink. "That hurts."

"Do you want to go to meet Aiden and show him how beautiful you look in the morning or would you rather look like you were just drooling into your pillow?"

"Can I choose drooling into my pillow?" I splashed my face with water and stared sadly at my lackluster appearance. "And you're a liar, I don't look beautiful."

"Yes, you do, and Aiden will think so as well."

"Yeah, right." I wrinkled my nose. "He didn't think I was beautiful last night."

"Of course he did. He kissed you, remember?"

"And then he left when I invited him to come and check out my room." I groaned as I remembered the rejection of the night before. "And when I say left, I mean, he ran out faster than a cheetah on crack."

"Cheetah's don't do crack," Liv said as if I were being serious.

"Maybe they do, maybe they don't," I said and put some moisturizer on my face. "Who knows what they do? All I can say is that Aiden left fast. As fast as the fastest animal on earth."

"Alice, stop being goofy. I'm sure he just realized he had to be at work early or something."

"Yeah, I guess." I sighed. "It's not like his job is all that important, though, that he would just have to leave."

"He's an attorney for a top law firm, Alice." Liv rolled her eyes. "He's not like us; he can't just call in whenever he wants and pretend to be sick and just watch movies all day."

"I guess." I sighed. "I just can't believe he has any interest in me if he left last night."

"He did kiss you."

"I know, but what's a kiss when you've been offered more? Maybe he only kissed me to be polite." My stomach churned as I thought about that prospect. Would he really have grabbed my waist and held me tight if he was just trying to be polite?

"Aiden doesn't do anything to be polite," Liv reminded me, and she was correct. I could remember a few different occasions where we'd asked Aiden to take us somewhere or do something with us when we were younger and he'd told us no, pretty point-blank. He hadn't cared that Liv had even been faking tears one time we'd asked him to take us to the zoo. He'd told us to go into the bathroom and look into the mirror and we'd see a rhino and a giraffe. And then he'd burst out laughing. I smiled to myself as I recalled how rude Aiden had always been. Liv was right. There was no way Aiden would have kissed me if he wasn't into it, even a little bit.

"I guess I'll come." I pouted my lips and applied my new pink lipstick and then some lipgloss. "But I'm not going to flirt with him or ask him out or make him jealous."

"Good. Just be sweet and casual." Liv nodded. "Let him think that you couldn't care less about seeing him or about that fact that he just left last night."

"I couldn't care less," I said and fluffed out my hair. "He's a jerk."

"Yeah, he is," Liv said emphatically.

"Oh, Liv." I giggled. "You're just saying that because I'm sad."

"I don't want you to be upset over stupid Aiden." She looked at me with large brown eyes.

"I know. It's awkward that I've fallen for your brother." I groaned. "Who does that?"

"I think it's quite common." Liv laughed. "Many women fall for their best friend's brother. I mean, it will be awesome if you guys end up together. We'd be sisters."

"See." I said with a sad face and pointed at her. "You have doubts, too."

"Doubts about what?"

"You just said *if* we end up together, not *when* we end up together."

"Oh." She bit her lower lip and looked to the side. "I didn't realize."

"It's fine," I said with a groan. "I mean, let's be realistic. You meet a guy and let him know you're interested and he's got you on the floor with his head between your legs. And I meet a man and let him know I'm interested and he gives me a quick snog and then darts off before I can even get him to the floor or the bed."

"A quick snog?" Liv giggled.

"I've been watching British TV shows again." I laughed. "I think snog sounds better than just saying kiss."

"At least you're not saying pash anymore." She laughed.

"What's wrong with pash?" I said indignantly. "I want to pash Aiden all night long."

"It just sounds weird."

"Tell that to an Australian," I said with a smirk. "They will most probably throw a kangaroo in your face."

"Yeah, let them try. I'll throw a koala bear back at them." She laughed. "I mean, who calls kissing pashing? It just doesn't even make sense to me."

"Pashing is a sexy term," I said, though I didn't really think it was that sexy. It was different, and to me different was cool.

"Are you still watching that show?"

"What show?"

"*Dating in the Dark Australia*?"

"Oh yeah." I nodded. "I thought you were talking about *Home and Away*."

"I thought you weren't able to watch it anymore?"

"Yeah, I'm not. The guy that was uploading it onto YouTube got deleted or something." I sighed. "That was a good show."

"It looked like too much drama to me. And all the characters seemed so young and annoying."

"Like I said, it was good." I laughed. "It was full of drama and angst and half the girls had worse love lives than me." I smiled happily, remembering all the drama from one of my favorite Australian soap operas. "Plus Australian men are so sexy."

"Oh, Alice, you and your English and Australian guys." Liv shook her head.

"I might end up marrying one if it doesn't work out with Aiden. Foreign guys are hotter."

"But then you'll have to move." Liv pouted.

"Yeah." I nodded. "I'll move to Oxfordshire or Sydney."

"Why Oxfordshire or Sydney?" Liv looked confused.

"Oh, they just sound like good places to live, if I have to leave the States."

"Uh, okay." I could see that Liv was trying not to laugh. "What about Nigeria?"

"What about Nigeria?" I frowned. What did Nigeria have to do with anything?

"Didn't a Nigerian prince ask you to marry him and send him ten thousand dollars?"

"Hahaha." I laughed slightly as I remembered the scam email I'd gotten and almost fallen for. "Very funny."

"Wouldn't you like to live in Nigeria as well?" she asked with a grin. "Seeing as you want to live abroad and all."

"I don't know about Nigeria." I made a face. "I've heard the Ivory Coast is beautiful, though."

"I guess you just have to meet a guy from there, then."

"Actually, there is a guy from there who's trying to buy a house right now. He has this sexy French accent as well." I thought about the tall African guy who always smiled at me when he came to see Mike, one of the agents at the real estate office I worked at. "I would definitely date him if he was younger than fifty." I giggled. "He's cute, but a bit old. But imagine if I lived in Africa, I'd be tan year round."

"You just want to leave me." Liv pouted again, and I laughed.

"Don't be silly. I want Aiden. I just need him to want me, too." I sighed and grabbed my handbag. "Are you ready?"

"Yeah, let's go." Liv linked arms with me. "I seriously need to make sure my brother doesn't mess this up."

"Yes, you do," I said expressively, with a small smile on my face. "Because if you don't, who knows where I'll end up?"

"You'll end up in Timbuktu, that's where." She laughed as we walked out of the door.

LIV AND I WALKED INTO the coffee shop, and I almost groaned when I saw Scott sitting there with Aiden. Why oh why did Scott have to be there? As if everything wasn't already slightly awkward between Aiden and me, Scott was just going to make an already complicated situation more complicated.

"Look who's here," Scott said with a grin as he jumped up and walked towards us. "Big ears and little ears."

"Look who's here," Liv retorted back. "Dumb and Dumber."

"I call Dumber," Scott said and then winked at me as he gave me a quick hug.

"I guess that leaves me as just Dumb?" Aiden said with a smile as he stood up and hugged Liv.

"Well, duh," Liv said as she pulled away from him. "We all knew you were dumb a long time ago."

"Touché," Aiden said as he walked towards me and gave me a quick hug, too. "Good to see you, Alice." His body felt warm next to me and I didn't want to let go as he stepped back. I know, I'm pathetic.

"Hi," I said and then a thought suddenly hit me. "I guess you didn't have to work early this morning?"

"No, did I say I had to?" He looked confused as he gazed at me and then at Liv. "Did I tell you I had to go to work early this morning?" he asked Liv and she made a face.

"No." She sighed. "Alice and I just got confused about something." She walked over to me. "What do you want, Alice? My treat."

"I'll have an iced mocha, please. Ooh, and a bagel with salmon and cream cheese."

"Okay." She nodded. "I'll be right back."

"Okay." I nodded and sat down. I swallowed hard as I saw both Aiden and Scott standing there in front of me.

"Well, Alice, how have you been?" Scott grinned and sat down next to me.

"Good, you?" I said weakly as I could feel Aiden's eyes on me.

"Good, just been working late." He stretched and I watched as he tossed his blond hair back. "I heard that you were at the parents' house recently?"

"Yeah, Liv wanted your dad to spend more time with Xander." I nodded. "Though, it was mainly the four of us just playing board games and going out."

"Sounds about right." Scott laughed. "Dad just likes having us all around the house. Unfortunately, Aiden and Liv are the only good kids. Chett and I rarely make an appearance."

"Aw, that's sad," I said and Scott leaned towards me with a small smile.

"I guess I would have made more of an effort had I known you were going to be there."

"Oh." I blushed at his words. I mean, what did you say to a man who was flirting with you when your crush was sitting right next to him?

"Maybe next time," Scott continued. "Or maybe we can go to—"

"Scott, Liv is calling you." Aiden cut him off with a brusque tone.

"Huh?" Scott looked at Aiden with a frown. "Calling me for what?"

"Go and ask her," Aiden said, his lips thin.

"Fine." Scott jumped up and then smiled at me. "We'll continue this conversation later."

"Okay," I said and avoided Aiden's stare.

"So what's going on with you and Scott?" he asked me accusingly and I looked at him with an annoyed expression.

"What do you mean what's going on with me and Scott?" I glared at him. Was he seriously going to go there? He was the one who had left me the previous evening.

"Do you like him?" he asked me point blank and I blinked slowly.

"Of course I like him," I said with an irritated tone.

"Do you want to date him?"

"No, I don't want to date him." I glared at him. I wanted to add *You big doofus* to my sentence, but didn't.

"Do you want to make out with him again?"

"We never made out. He kissed me. Once," I said, my voice getting higher. "I didn't ask him to kiss me."

"But you didn't stop him." He frowned. "You seem to like kissing us Taylor brothers, don't you?"

"I don't like kissing the Taylor brothers, no." I bit my lower lip and took a deep breath. "I only liked kissing one of the Taylor brothers."

"Oh?" He froze and his eyes held mine.

"Yes," I said, feeling light in the head. Was I seriously going to tell him how I felt, right here and now?

"Which one?" he asked and leaned towards me, so that I could see his pupils dilating."

"I like—"

"There you are, darling." A soft sweet voice echoed next to us and I looked up in shock. There, standing next to us in the flesh, was Elizabeth Jeffries. What was she doing here?

"Lizzie!" Aiden jumped up and beamed, his face transforming from a slightly angry mask to one of pure happiness.

"Sorry I'm late." She wrinkled her nose, and even I had to admit that she looked cute while doing so.

"You're not late. You're right on time," he said and gave her a quick hug and a kiss on the cheek. I wanted to burst into tears at the sight of the two of them together. "Elizabeth, I want you to meet Alice. Alice is my sister Liv's best friend." He nodded towards me. "And Alice, I want you to meet Elizabeth, a good friend of mine."

"Hi." I nodded at her, and she gave me a wide, genuine smile. I couldn't stop myself from studying her. Her nose was a little crooked and she had freckles across her cheeks. Her hair was a honey blond, but as I studied her dark eyebrows, I was pretty sure she dyed it. She looked prettier in person than she had in the photos, and I hated her for it.

"Nice to meet you, Alice," she said cheerfully and leaned down for a quick hug. "I've heard so much about you."

"You have?" I asked in surprise. Did Aiden talk about me?

"Yes, Aiden's always talking about his sister and her best friend and all the funny things you both do."

"All the funny things we both do?" I questioned and then looked at Aiden. What had he been telling her?

"Like the pranks and stuff." Elizabeth smiled. "Like Brock and Jock, the strippers you paid to pretend to be your boyfriends."

"I see." I frowned. Why was Aiden telling her this stuff?

"I think that your plan was ingenious," she continued and sat down next to me. "And it worked."

"It did?" I looked at her questioningly.

"Well, Liv got the boy, didn't she?"

"Yeah, I guess so." I nodded and sighed. "Yeah, I guess it did end up working for Liv."

"I can't wait to meet her." Elizabeth smiled at me and my heart thudded as I realized that she was a completely genuine and nice person. She was the sort of person who I'd have as a friend if she weren't trying to steal my man away from me.

"Yeah, I'm sure Liv wants to meet you as well." I turned away from her and looked at Aiden. "You didn't tell me your girlfriend was coming."

"Uhm, Elizabeth isn't my girlfriend," Aiden said with a pleasant look, but his eyes never left my face.

"Yeah, we're not dating," Elizabeth interjected. "We've only gone out a few times."

"Do you know where Aiden was last night?" I said pettily and immediately regretted it. Who was I becoming? Why was I acting like this? I knew I was letting my jealousy get the better of me and I didn't like it.

"No, should I?" Elizabeth asked with a small laugh and then looked up at Aiden. "Where were you last night?"

"I was at Liv's place watching a movie with Alice," he replied nonchalantly and smiled at me. I glared back at him. What game was he playing?

"Oh, awesome. What movie?" she asked and I wondered how she could be so trusting. If a guy I was seeing told me he'd gone to watch a movie with another woman, I would not be smiling and taking it this nicely. In fact, if I were dating Aiden officially and he had told me that he had gone to watch a movie with Elizabeth, I would have let him know exactly what I thought about him. I don't play around, and I certainly do not let my guys go on dates with other girls. And yes, I know, last night hadn't exactly been a date. However, we had kissed and I'd been on his lap and he'd been hard for me. I'd felt his hardness on my ass. And yes, I had tried my best to get him excited, but I hadn't made him rise to the occasion. He had done that himself. I knew that if Aiden had gotten hard for another girl while dating me, it would have been over.

"I can't remember," I said and looked down, suddenly feeling guilty. Why was she so nice and why was I so horrible? Why did I feel like the other woman?

"That good, huh?" She laughed and we both looked up as Scott and Liv approached the table. I watched Elizabeth's eyes widen as she gazed at Scott and his eyes narrowed as he gazed at her. I almost wondered if I'd imagined the exchange because within seconds they were both smiling normally and Aiden was making introductions.

Liv and I made eye contact, and I could tell that she looked as confused as I did when Elizabeth had arrived. We were both thinking, *why was this girl here?* And she was totally ruining our plan of me making Aiden want me. How could I make Aiden want me if there was another girl with him right now? Why would he even care about me? And why was he acting so funny about Scott if he had Elizabeth? Maybe it was a simple case of wanting what you didn't really want because you couldn't have it. All of a sudden, I felt really sorry for myself.

"Excuse me, but I'm not feeling well," I said and stood up. My head was pounding and my insides felt empty. All of a sudden I felt tired, really, really tired.

"What's wrong, Alice?" Liv looked at me with wide eyes. I think she could tell from my face that I was close to tears.

"Nothing, maybe I'm coming down with a cold." I attempted a cough and looked at the group. "I'm going to go home." I looked at Elizabeth and smiled weakly. "It was nice meeting you."

"You too." She looked nervous and worried as she smiled at me, and I saw her look at Aiden a few times. I looked over at him and his face looked expressionless. I had no idea what he was thinking.

"I'll walk you home," Scott said, and I watched as Aiden frowned.

"Thanks," I said gratefully, not caring what Aiden thought at this point.

"Do you want me to come?" Liv said, and I shook my head.

"No, no. You stay. I'm fine." I gave her a weak smile and rubbed my head. "I'll see you later, okay?"

"Okay." She nodded and sat down.

"Ready?" Scott said and grabbed my hand. "Lean on me, I'll help you."

"Thanks," I said gratefully and hurried away from the table. We walked out of the coffee shop fairly quickly, and I took a deep breath of fresh air as we walked along the street.

"You okay, Alice?" Scott stopped and pulled me over to the side of the street. His eyes searched mine, and he had a small smile on his face.

"Yes, why?" I asked softly.

"I'm not going to pretend to know what's going through your head," he said as he gazed at me. "But I am going to give you some advice. You need to fight for what you want. You need to grab life by the horns and go after your dreams and goals."

"What are you talking about?" I said and swallowed hard.

"I know you like Aiden." He gave me a half-smile and shook his head. "I don't know why you prefer him to me, but I know you do."

"I, uh …" I stammered. I wasn't sure what to say to him. Had I been in a love triangle and not even known it? That would be just my luck. I didn't want to be in a love triangle. Not at all. Not with any percentage of my being. How icky would that make me to be in a love triangle with two brothers? Granted, I had kissed both of them, but let's be real, I didn't really consider my kiss with Scott anything other than a brief peck. I'd regretted it as it happened. I certainly hadn't kissed him back. And there was no tongue involved. Thank God! So really, it wasn't even a kiss. What sort of kiss doesn't involve tongue?

"There's no need for you to say anything." Scott laughed and we continued walking again. "I'm just saying you need to fight for what you want. And if you want Aiden, you have to let him know. Without the games. And without the tricks." He reached forward and patted me on the nose. "I know you and my sister love to play games and stuff, but Aiden's not the guy for that sort of thing. He doesn't have patience for games or tricks."

"I don't have a shot with him anyway," I said with a sigh. "He has Elizabeth."

"I wouldn't be so sure about that." Scott's eyes narrowed and he looked thoughtful. "I'm not sure exactly what Aiden and Elizabeth have going on, but I don't think it's a regular relationship."

"Oh, you think it could be something other than a regular relationship?" My mind immediately went to BDSM. Was Elizabeth his sub?

"I don't know." Scott shrugged, and we both stopped once we reached my building. "You going to be okay? I should get going, I have some work to do."

"Yeah, sure." I nodded and tried to stop myself from asking if he knew his older brother was a Dom. It wasn't my place to bring that up. "I'll be fine. Thanks for walking me home."

"It was my pleasure, Alice. It was my pleasure." Scott gave me a quick hug and I hurried through the front door and up to my apartment. I'd gone and made a mess of everything. I felt horrible. Here I was feeling upset and jealous about Aiden and Elizabeth and now there was a possibility that I'd gone and made Scott fall for me as well.

I WOKE UP TO MY phone buzzing and groaned. I hadn't meant to fall back asleep. I'd just wanted to lie down and relax and think about everything for a few seconds. I grabbed my phone and looked at the screen and my heart skipped a beat. Aiden had texted me.

Aiden: *Hey, just checking that you're okay.*

Alice: *I'm fine. Thank you,* I typed back quickly as I sat up in the bed. I wanted to ask him where Elizabeth was, but I didn't dare.

Aiden: *We never got to finish our conversation.*

Alice: *Oh, we didn't?*

Aiden: *No. Can we chat later?*

Alice: *Aren't you going to be busy?*

Aiden: *Busy with what?*

Alice: *Work,* I typed, even though that wasn't what I was talking about.

Aiden: *I don't have to be in court today.*

Alice: *Okay.* That's not what I was talking about!

Aiden: *So are you available to chat?*

Alice: *What time?*

Aiden: *Whenever you're free is good with me.*

Alice: *I see.*

Aiden: *Unless you're going to be busy.*

Alice: *With what?*

Aiden: *Scott.*

My jaw dropped. I couldn't believe that he had actually typed that.

Aiden: *So will you be free or busy?*

Alice: *I'm free. There is nothing between Scott and me.*

Aiden: *Good.*

Alice: *Why good?*

Aiden: *You don't need to be playing games with Scott and myself.*

Alice: *What about you and Elizabeth?* I couldn't stop myself.

Aiden: *What about her?*

Alice: *How can you date her and kiss me?*

Aiden: *That is part of the reason why we need to talk.*

Alice: *I see.*

Aiden: *Can I call you now?*

Alice: *No, I'm busy,* I lied as I lay back in my pillows.

Aiden: *Okay, so tonight?*

Alice: *What about tomorrow?*

Aiden: *Alice, I swear to God you're the most confusing girl I've ever met.*

Alice: *I don't think you're confusing.*

Aiden: *If I was there I'd put you over my knee and spank you.*

Alice: *You'd like that, wouldn't you?*

Aiden: *I think you'd like it more.*

Alice: *Do you now?* I grinned at the phone. There was no doubt in my mind now. Aiden was definitely a kink-master in the bedroom.

Aiden: *I guess we'll have to wait and see.*

Alice: *And you're calling me confusing?* I shook my head at the phone. Everything in me was telling me that he was flirting with me.

Aiden: *I wouldn't be confusing if it wasn't for you.*

Alice: *What does that mean?*

Aiden: *It means that you my dear, Alice have affected me much more than you think.*

Alice: *Oh? How?*

Aiden: *You'll have to wait to find out.*

Alice: *Okay.* I was itching to tell him to just call me now. I wished that he would just call me and be done with it.

Aiden: *Have a good day.*

Alice: *Thanks, you too.* Was that it? Argh. I was irritated that he was just going to stop chatting when it was getting good.

Aiden: *I'll see you tomorrow at flag football.*

Alice: *Ok.* Wait, what? Was he calling me tonight or not?

Aiden: *I'm glad you're feeling better.*

Alice: *Thank you.*

Aiden: *You need to take better care of yourself.*

Alice: *I do.*

Aiden: *Get eight hours of sleep and eat your veggies.*

Alice: *Yes, Dad.*

Aiden: *There are better nicknames you can call me.*

Alice: *Like what?*

Aiden: *You'll see.*

Alice: *Like Sir?* I typed and laughed, wondering what his face looked like as he read the message.

Alice: *Or Master?* I typed again and waited for his response.

Aiden: *Whatever you like. :)*

Alice: *Aiden Taylor!!*

Aiden: *That works as well! :)*

Alice: *Fine. Whatever. See you tomorrow.*

Aiden: *Yes. And we'll chat after.*

Alice: *We'll see,* I typed, feeling annoyed.

Aiden: *Have a good day, Alice. I know I will. My lips are still tingling from your kisses last night.*

Alice: *I hope you didn't catch anything.*

Aiden: *Is there something you need to tell me?*

Oops. I guess my quick-witted diss was really a diss to myself.

Alice: *Funny. Not.*

Aiden: *Call me if you need anything.*

Alice: *Thanks. I will.* I put my phone down on the bed and lay back and stared at the ceiling. All of a sudden I felt better. Confused still, but better.

Maybe Aiden really did like me. And maybe I really did have a chance. Maybe, just maybe, I could let him see that he was the one for me and I was the one for him. I just hoped that Elizabeth Jeffries would just disappear, along with my insecurities.

EIGHT

Football is a dance of seduction

THE BEST FEELING IN THE world is when a guy you like likes you. The second best feeling in the world is when another guy likes you and makes that guy jealous. The only part that can make these best feelings the worst feelings in the world is if you also like the second guy. There is nothing worse than being attracted to two guys and having them both like you. Trust me, I know. Well, I guess I'm stretching that a bit. I don't know if they both *like* me, like me. And I don't really *like* like both of them. I *really* like one of them and the other one just makes me feel good; and that might not even be because he likes me. I don't really know, if I'm honest. What I do know is that they both act like they kinda like me when I see them on the football field. And yeah, what does that really mean? There are so many men who like to flirt just for flirting's sake. It doesn't mean they actually like you.

"HOW DO YOU ASK A man to dominate you?" I whispered to Liv as we made our way onto the field. "How do you bring that up casually?"

"It seems like he might already know that you want that," Liv said as she gazed at me with a huge grin.

"Well, I don't think he does."

"I wish you would let me tell Xander that I know about Aiden." She made a face and I squeezed her arm hard.

"No, you can't tell him that I told you. He'll never trust me again."

"Trust you with what?"

"Anything." I moaned. "I don't want him to think I have a big mouth."

"He has to know you'd tell me." Liv frowned. "I can't even believe that he wants to keep this a secret from me."

"He doesn't want to scar you."

"I am a big girl. It will take more than finding out my brother is a freak in the bedroom to scar me."

"He's not a freak."

"I don't mean *freak* freak." She laughed. "I meant freaky freak."

"Haha, so are you going to call me freaky as well?" I questioned her with a smile.

"Why would I call you freaky?"

"If I became Aiden's sub?"

"Number one, I can't see you as a sub, but whatever floats your boat. Just don't wear a choker, please." She groaned. "No chokers with studs, they look so tacky."

"What looks tacky?" Henry ran over to us with a big smile and lifted his hand up so I could high-five him.

"Choker necklaces," Liv said and made a face.

"Oh, I haven't seen a woman in one of those since ..." His voice trailed off and he winked at us. "Well, since a fun night I had a few years ago."

"What sort of fun night?" I asked curiously and I watched as Henry licked his lips and laughed.

"Trust me, girls, you don't want to know."

"Everyone gather around, please." Aiden's voice was loud and booming, and I noticed that he didn't even glance in my direction as he spoke.

"Someone's upset the bear," Henry said with a laugh and looked at me.

"Not me," I said and made a face.

"It's always you, Alice," Liv said with a grin. "It's always you."

"RUN ALICE, RUN!" LIV SCREAMED as I ran down the field with the ball in my hands. I was in shock as I held it close to my body and continued dashing down the field. I could see the marking lines that Aiden had spray painted in the grass, even though I was pretty sure that they were against the rules of the park. That had shocked me because Aiden was someone who never broke the rules.

"Keep going, Alice!" Liv screamed, and I made the mistake of looking back. Scott was a few feet away from me, and Henry was close behind him. I was praying that Henry got to Scott before Scott got to me. I could also see Aiden coming up fast behind Henry, and Elizabeth was farther back on the field near Xander and Liv. I gasped for air as I turned back around. I could see one of the guys on my team signaling to me to throw him the ball, but I didn't want to pass the game-winning touchdown to some guy whose name I didn't even know. I wanted to be the MVP of the game. I didn't want the guys to just look at Liv and me as two silly girls with no business being on the field. We weren't like Elizabeth: we didn't run marathons; we didn't play pickup basketball at the Y; and we weren't hiking up mountains or surfing in the Pacific Ocean along the coast of one of the Hawaiian Islands. We were just average, regular girls who liked to have fun and played sports for some excitement in our lives. I knew the guys thought we were pretty worthless on the field, especially me. I mean, I couldn't blame them. I wasn't in the best shape, but I knew if I scored this touchdown and scored the winning points, I'd be looked at with new eyes. This was about the game. In this moment, I didn't care about Aiden or Scott or Henry or whatever other guy might be interested in me. I didn't care about looking pretty or sexy. I didn't care about being witty. I didn't care about making Aiden jealous. All I cared about was winning. And I knew that in this moment, for the first time in my life, I was a sportswoman. A true, dedicated and fearless sportswoman. I kept my head down and ignored the pain in my stomach and the cramps in my legs. I was not going to slow down. I was not going to let the pain win. I was nearly there.

"You've nearly got it, Alice!" Liv screamed, and I charged forward. I felt a hand grazing my back and I knew that Scott nearly had me.

"Oh no you don't!" I screamed and threw my body forward as I saw the line Aiden had made right in front of me. "Touchdown!" I screamed as I fell to the ground and hit the ball against the grass. "Touchdown!" I screamed again in excitement, tears and sweat pouring down my face.

"Move over, Alice!" Scott groaned as he came charging towards me.

"What?" My body was frozen in shock as he came crashing down on me, his body feeling like a ton of bricks as he fell forward. "Ow!" I cried out, as my already aching bones screamed out in pain. His knees nudged my stomach painfully, and I cried out again. "Ooww!" I moaned as he looked over at me.

"Nice touchdown." He grinned down at me, his blue eyes sparkling as he wiped mud off of his face.

"Thank you," I said lightly and tried to push him off of me.

"Oh, sorry." He laughed and jumped up. "I guess you can say you're a seasoned player now."

"I guess so." I groaned as I tried to stand up. "Ugh." I moaned and grabbed my knee. "I think I cut myself."

"We won! We won!" Liv screamed and grinned as she came running towards me. "We're the champions, Alice!"

"Yay." I smiled and groaned again, as the pain in my knee got worse and worse.

"What's wrong?" Suddenly Aiden was in front of me, his face looking grim.

"I hurt my knee," I said in a low voice. "And no need to be pissed, because we won."

"I'm not pissed," he said with a frown and kneeled down to the ground. "I'm going to pull your pants leg up so I can check your knee, okay?"

I nodded mutely and watched as he pulled the right leg of my exercise pants up. We both stared at my bloody knee, and I groaned.

"Oh my God, I'm injured." I frowned and Aiden looked at me with a concerned face.

"Are you okay?"

"She's fine," Scott said and rolled his eyes. "Just scraped her knee."

"Have some compassion, Scott!" Liv snapped and walked over to me. "You okay, Alice?"

"I'm fine. I guess I just need to clean it."

"See, she's fine." Scott laughed and then looked at me. "I promise that our next rumble and tumble in the grass won't leave you with any injuries."

"There won't be another rumble and tumble," Aiden growled and put my arm around his shoulder. "Lean on me and I'm going to help you stand up."

"Okay," I said softly.

"I have a first-aid kit in my car, so I'll clean it for you."

"Okay. Thank you." I smiled at him sweetly, and I could see Liv grinning. I looked towards Scott, and he winked at me and then wiggled his eyebrows towards Aiden. I realized then that Scott was no longer interested in me. Instead, he was helping to make Aiden jealous. I giggled to myself as I realized that he was just as bad as I was, but I knew he was doing it for me, so I couldn't be mad at him.

"Are you okay, Alice?" Elizabeth walked up to us with a look of concern on her face.

"Yes, thanks." I nodded, feeling a bit bad. I was stealing her man from right under her nose. Not that he was really her beau or anything.

"Good. Excellent touchdown, by the way. Best move of the day!" Elizabeth grinned at me. "You sure showed the guys what's what."

"I try." I grinned back at her and for a second I felt guilty. Guilty that I was swooping Aiden out from under her when she really was a nice girl.

"Hey, hey, hey, what about my touchdown?" Scott looked at Elizabeth. "I think that my catch was pretty impressive."

"Impressive to whom?" She laughed and shook her head.

"Everyone on the field."

"Hmm, if you say so," she said and flipped her hair. I stared at her face and I was pretty sure she was blushing. Curious, I looked at Scott a bit closer. His face was positively beaming as he stared at her.

"I do say so." He moved closer to her. "Didn't you see me?"

"I saw you, and I saw Alice too, and Alice definitely had the move of the day."

"Hmmm." Scott looked back at me. "Maybe I'll concede this once."

"Wow, how grand of you." She laughed and patted the front of her T-shirt down. I was about to look away when I noticed something on her wrists. My eyes narrowed as I stared at the lines on her wrists.

"Are you ready, Alice?" Aiden's voice was close to my ear and I nodded.

"Yes." I glanced up at him, and he put his left arm around me and pulled me up easily. I loved the fact that he was acting as if I were some hundred-pound lightweight and not the considerable amount more that I really was.

"Can you walk or do you need me to carry you?" he asked me as I leaned into him. I looked at his face to see if he was teasing me, but he looked quite serious. For a split second, I wanted to tell him that I needed him to carry me. I wanted to start limping and moaning and making out like I was really hurt, but I didn't. And not because I'm above faking an injury to get close to a guy, but because I knew it wouldn't be believable. He'd seen my injury. I had scraped the skin off of my knee and it was bleeding. It wasn't a serious injury. Yes, it stung a bit, and yes, I was feeling slightly woozy, but I wasn't in need of him carrying me. At least, not because of the injury I'd sustained. If he were offering to carry me into his bedroom, I would have had a completely different answer.

"I'm fine. I don't need you to carry me."

"Pity," he said softly and I looked over at him in surprise. His face still looked serious and I wondered if I had imagined him saying those words. We walked towards his car in companionable silence, and I enjoyed the feeling of his warm body next to me as he led me across the field. "I know I told you I wanted to talk to you, but you didn't have to injure yourself to get my attention," he said as we reached his car.

"I didn't," I said smugly. "I don't need to injure myself to get attention."

"True, you don't." He laughed.

"What's so funny?" My eyes narrowed as I gazed at him laughing down at me.

"I was just thinking about all the other ways that you draw attention to yourself."

"Oh?"

"Like saying you want to be a lingerie model at Victoria's Secret."

"I never said that!" I shook my head. "Henry said that."

"But you sure seemed happy when he brought it up."

"What are you talking about?" I shook my head and got into the backseat of his car.

"It seems to me you want men to think about you parading about in lingerie."

"No, I don't." I shook my head and watched as he slid into the backseat next to me. "Why would you even think that?"

"Maybe because that's all I've been able to think about for the last week?"

"What? My conversation with Henry?"

"No, you goof." He opened his center console and took out his first-aid kit. "You in lingerie."

"Me in lingerie?" I breathed out and watched as he pulled up the leg of my pants again so that he could clean my wound.

"Yes, that's all I've been thinking about for the last week."

"That's very bold of you to say." I gasped as he placed the antiseptic lotion on my knee.

"Why?" He looked up into my eyes as his fingers rubbed against my skin.

"Because."

"Because what?"

"Just because." I moaned as his lips came dangerously close to mine. "What are you doing?"

"What do you want me to be doing?"

"Aiden," I groaned, and he chuckled and moved back.

"I thought you liked kissing me. You liked kissing me last week."

"I don't understand you, Aiden," I groaned and watched as he put a Band-Aid on my knee and leaned down to kiss it.

"All better," he said and looked at me. "What do you want to understand?"

"What were the marks on Elizabeth's wrists?" I asked quickly, the words darting out of my mouth before I could stop them.

"The marks on Elizabeth's wrists?" He raised an eyebrow at me. "What marks?"

"She had red indents on her wrists," I said. "I saw them. They looked like ..." My voice trailed off before I could say the words 'handcuff marks'.

"They looked like what?" He grinned and leaned towards me, his lashes looking longer then I remembered.

"You know." I swallowed hard. How could I ask him what sort of relationship they had together?

"No, I don't."

"They looked like handcuff marks," I said finally.

"Oh, really?" He smiled and licked his lips deliberately.

"Yes."

"You're asking me if Elizabeth had handcuff marks on her wrists?"

"I'm asking you if you're seeing her, like, properly," I said, no longer able to hold it in. "I don't think it's cool if you are seeing her and seeing me at the same time."

"I'm seeing you?" he asked with a smirk and his eyes fell to my lips.

"Well, you know," I said, feeling like a fool. Why had I said he was seeing me? He wasn't seeing me. All we'd done was kiss.

"No, I didn't know." He laughed and pulled away suddenly and slid out of the car. "Come on." He grabbed my hands and pulled me out to join him.

"I didn't mean to say you were seeing both of us," I mumbled as I stood next to him. The sunlight was blinding me, and I stared at his shoulder, instead of into his eyes.

"That's good."

"I mean, I guess you are dating her, but you aren't dating me."

"I am?" he asked.

"Well, aren't you?" I asked and shifted my eyes to look into his. Aiden put his arms around my waist and pulled me into him.

"Do you want to be dating me, Alice?" he asked softly and my breath caught.

"I, uh, I ..." I stammered, my face red and not just from the direct rays of sun on my skin.

"I liked kissing you the other night," he said softly with a small smile and leaned down. "Did you like kissing me?"

"Yes," I squeaked out.

"Good." He leaned down and gave me a quick kiss on the lips. "You and me are having dinner tonight and we're going to talk."

"We are?" I squeaked out again, this time in a more indignant manner.

"Yes, we are." He kissed me again, this time harder and for longer.

"You didn't even ask."

"I learned my lesson yesterday," he said with his lips against mine. "I asked you if I could call you, and you gave me the run around. Today, I figure there's no point in me just asking you. I need to tell you."

"Well, I don't know what to say," I said breathlessly, my lips brushing against his.

"Just tell me what time to pick you up." He sucked on my lower lip and tugged gently. "Actually, I'll pick you up at eight."

"Oh." My stomach was doing flips and I put my hands around his waist to stop myself from reaching down to grab his ass.

"Be ready." He laughed and pulled my face towards him and gave me one deep, hard kiss before pulling back.

"Or what?"

"Or you'll see." He winked.

"You going to punish me?" I asked lightly, and he just laughed. I saw the others waiting for us in the field and so I started walking towards them. I wondered if they had seen us kissing and if they had, what were they thinking? I sure hoped Elizabeth didn't think that she had anything serious with Aiden. I sure hoped that they didn't have anything that would prevent me from working my magic. I also hoped that they hadn't kissed or had sex. Though I didn't want to ask. I didn't want to know if they had, only if they hadn't. And how did you ask that question knowing that one of the answers had the potential to break your heart?

"I can't wait for tonight," Aiden said from behind me and I jumped as I felt his hand lightly tapping my ass.

"Hey!" I turned around and glared at him. "What was that for?"

"I was just answering your question," He said and ran ahead of me. My heart thudded as I realized that tonight might involve a lot more than just talking.

SEDUCTION IS LIKE A DANCE. You have to move in time, at the right moment, and just let yourself go. I stared at my reflection in the mirror. I looked sexy. Or as sexy as I could look without having a professional stylist and makeup artist at my beck and call. No one can ever say I'm a quitter. Nope, not me. When Aiden asked me if I wanted to get dinner, I thought I was going to faint. And I mean that quite literally. My body felt weak and my heart was racing. I could hear the humming of birds in my ear and everything in my world was bright and wonderful. All because Aiden asked me to dinner. I know, I'm a bit of a sad case, but that's what it's like when a guy you like asks you out. It's magical. Absolutely magical.

I grabbed my handbag as the clock on the wall turned to eight and then I stopped for a few seconds to make sure I was ready.

Red heels. Check.

Sexy underwear. Check.

Handcuffs. Check.

Aiden waiting for me naked in his large king-sized bed with nothing but a sexy smile on his face. I hoped that would be a check real soon. Like tonight soon. I was so excited I could barely contain myself. I checked my handbag to make sure I had my box of condoms (I wasn't going to let protection be the one thing that prevented me from getting down and dirty tonight). I had my red lipstick that matched my heels perfectly. I had some strawberry lipgloss. I had a small bottle of Vera Wang's Princess perfume because it made me smell divine. I was going to spray myself with it again once I got to the restaurant because the scent never seemed to last long. I had a pack of Altoids mints because I wanted to make sure I had fresh breath and I knew a good blowjob trick with Altoids in your mouth. I also had my cellphone. Forty dollars in cash. My driver's license, in case I got carded when ordering my cocktails. And I also had a small teddy bear that I always carried around with me. It was a bear that Aiden had given me when I was a little kid and he had won it at a fair. He probably didn't even remember that he'd given me that prize, so many years ago, but I made sure to carry it with me everywhere. It was one of my prized possessions. Sometimes when I was in bed, late at night and feeling lonely, I would grab that teddy bear and squeeze it and kiss it and hold it close and imagine that somehow it was making me close to Aiden. It was a juvenile thing to do, but it was something that always comforted me.

"He's here, Alice!" Liv screamed down the corridor. "I saw his car pull up."

"How do I look?" I hurried out of my room in my short black dress and Liv whistled.

"Uhm, hotter than the Sahara Desert."

"Hotter, huh?" I grinned and twirled around in my dress. "I feel pretty hot."

"You're more than pretty hot, you're super-hot." She laughed and came over to me. She poked her finger into my arm and screeched.

"What's wrong?" I asked her with a confused frown.

"You're so hot you just burned me." She grinned and we both burst out laughing.

"You're a goof," I said. "It's a good thing you're not a man. You'd never get laid with pickup lines like that."

"I think I'd make a good man," she said with a smile. "I'd know exactly what to say to get the girls."

"Uh huh." I grinned, and she looked me up and down slowly and licked her lips.

"Man, girl, you look good enough to eat." She paused and licked her lips again. "And I'm hungry, you wanna show me some sugar?"

"Oh my God, no, just no!" I started laughing again. "You will never get a woman with words like that. No to the no, to the hell, to the no."

"Haha, that bad?" She grinned at me and then laughed. "Yeah, that was pretty bad. Thank God, I'm a woman and have Xander."

"Yeah, you lucked out with Mr. Miracle Tongue." I smiled. "Smooth with his words and his tongue."

"Well, not always smooth with either." She winked and I groaned.

"Liv!"

"What?" She laughed. "I'm being honest. He's not always smooth. Sometimes he's rough and bumpy."

"Liv, TMI." I groaned again and then froze as the doorbell rang. He was here. Aiden was finally here and I was going on what I thought was my first official date with him. I wanted to scream. "Liv, I think I'm going to faint," I said, my throat suddenly dry.

"Why?" She looked concerned. "Do you need some water?"

"I'm going on a date with Aiden," I groaned yet again as the doorbell rang another time. "Why is he so impatient?"

"Because he's Aiden." She rolled her eyes. "He has the patience of a dog."

"I guess I'd better go and let him in."

"Yeah, do that before he bangs the door down." She made a face and then gave me a sweet smile. "You really do look gorgeous though, Alice. Aiden is lucky to be able to take you out."

"Thanks, Liv," I said and hurried to the front door. I opened it quickly to find Aiden standing there with his hand in the air. "You weren't about to ring the doorbell again, were you?"

"I was." He smiled and looked me up and down, his eyes widening as his gaze fell to my tall red heels. "You look nice tonight, Alice."

"That's it?" Liv walked over to the front door. "She looks *nice*?"

"Yes, she looks nice." Aiden looked at Liv with an annoyed expression. "Don't you think so?"

"Alice looks bloody gorgeous," Liv said and shook her head. "Like a million bucks."

"Thanks, Liv." I laughed and I could see Aiden shaking his head at his sister.

"Yes, Alice, you do look beautiful tonight." He reached his hand forward. "Very, very beautiful."

"That's more like it," Liv said, and he groaned.

"Alice, are you ready to go?" Aiden muttered. "I'm afraid if I have to listen to my sister anymore tonight, I might go crazy."

"I don't have time to drive you crazy tonight, dear brother. Xander is taking me out to dinner as well." Liv smiled at her brother and then continued. "And I know he's taking me to a nice restaurant, not a Burger King."

"More the fool him, then," Aiden joked, and Liv glared at him.

"Let's go," I said and turned around to give Liv a quick hug. "See you later."

"Bye, don't do anything I wouldn't do," she said, and I quickly opened my handbag and let her see the contents. "Or maybe not." She giggled as she saw the handcuffs.

"What are you two giggling about now?" Aiden said with an interested expression, but I quickly closed my handbag again and turned back towards him.

"Nothing," I said innocently and hurried out of the front door. "Let's go and eat. I'm starving."

"I'm feeling pretty hungry too," he said, and I felt his hand slip around my waist as we made our way out of the building. "I'm just not sure what I'll get to eat yet."

We made our way to his car, and Aiden hurried forward so that he could open the passenger door to his what appeared to be a new black Mercedes C300. "Not driving your Lincoln Navigator anymore?" I asked in surprise.

"No, it's at home."

"Oh, so this is a second car?" I raised an eyebrow at him. He had a Lincoln and a Mercedes now?

"Yeah." He nodded and then closed the door after I slid into the luxurious tan leather seat. It felt plush and warm against my bare legs, and I sank back into the seat with a happy smile on my face.

"Why did you get another car?" I asked him as he got behind the driver's seat.

"Because I wanted to." He shrugged. "Why? Don't you like Mercedes?"

"They seem fine. I've never been in one before."

"Oh. They're very smooth." He turned on the engine and looked over at me. "Hear how it purrs for me?"

"No, not really." I shook my head, and he put his hand to his ear and growled.

"You don't hear that?"

"No, and thank God. If I heard that sound coming from your engine, I wouldn't still be in your car."

"Touché." He laughed. "Okay, are you ready to eat?"

"I've been ready."

"How is your knee?" His right hand reached down and touched my leg. My skin tingled as his fingertips gently brushed across my skin and to my kneecap.

"It's okay. It tingles a bit, but it will be okay."

"Good." His fingers moved back up my leg and up my thigh, and my breath caught as they worked their way towards the middle of my leg. "I love your dress, by the way," he said and moved his fingers back to the steering wheel.

"Thank you," I said and looked over at him. "You look very dapper in your shirt and tie."

"I'm glad you appreciate the tie."

"I always appreciate a tie," I said, and he looked at me with a smile.

"In all circumstances."

"Yes," I said, barely breathing as he gazed at me.

"Good." He changed the gears suddenly and pulled out into the street.

"Where are we going?" I asked him as we zipped along the road with the other cars.

"I figured I'd take you out for a nice steak dinner," he said as I adjusted in the seat and fiddled with the radio. "Anything but Top 40, please."

"What's wrong with Top 40? I love Top 40."

"I don't need to hear Katy Perry or Beyoncé screeching in my ear about how they love being single."

"They don't screech. And they aren't single." I rolled my eyes at him. I stopped on a country music station and looked at him. "Is this better?"

"Nope. I don't want to hear about anyone taking their dog and their pickup truck to the lake to get over their ex."

"That's horrible." I laughed. "Not every country music song is about pickup trucks."

"There's enough for me to veto this station."

"What about this one?" I stopped it on a Spanish station and we listened to a man singing his heart out.

"I have no idea what he's saying." Aiden frowned. "Something about balancing?"

"No, he's talking about dancing." I laughed. "*Bailamos* is what he's saying, not balancing. *Bailamos* doesn't even sound like balancing."

"Hmm, I don't mind listening to this station if you're going to continue talking to me in Spanish."

"Oh?" I asked him curiously. "All I said was *bailamos*."

"And you sounded sexy saying it. I have a thing for Spanish accents."

"My accent isn't even that good."

"It's good enough, my sexy señorita."

"Oh, Aiden." I rolled my eyes.

"Say Aiiiden." He drawled out his name as he said it with an accent.

"Or maybe I'll call you Juan."

"You can call me whatever you want, señorita."

"You're an idiot," I said, and we both laughed.

"Seriously, though. I'm glad you came to dinner with me tonight."

"It's not like you really gave me a choice," I said. "It was more of an order."

"Well, thanks for obeying orders."

"You're welcome," I said, and he reached over and squeezed my hand.

"So I wanted to talk about the—" he said at the same time that I said "What's going on with you and Elizabeth?"

"So I guess we're both ready to talk, then?" He looked at me with a smile. "What did you want to talk about first?"

"What were you going to say?"

"I wanted to talk to you about that night you came to my room."

"Oh, again."

"I wanted you to know that I don't want to be your best friend's creepy older brother."

"You're not creepy at all."

"Sometimes I think I am." His voice sounded frustrated. "You and Liv have been best friends for so long, and I don't want you to think that I'm trying to horn in on that relationship."

"Aiden, I don't know if you remember, but I was the one who snuck into your bed. Not the other way around," I said with a small laugh. "I was the one who wanted you."

"I wasn't sure if I'd led you on."

"How had you led me on?" I asked curiously.

"You know, when I used to tutor you," he said and glanced at me before switching lanes.

"You mean when you tutored me for math?" I thought back to when I was in ninth grade and he'd spent a summer helping me figure out pre-calc and algebra.

"Yeah. And helped you figure out how to kiss." His voice dropped. "I still feel guilty about that."

"Why?" I looked at him in shock; I was surprised that he'd even remembered those days.

"I was your first kiss." He sighed. "And the first guy you slept with. I kinda felt like an asshole."

"Aiden, you were my first kiss, and you were amazing." I laughed. "If anything, I was the asshole. I was the one who practically forced you to teach me how to kiss."

"You didn't force me."

"I begged you for two weeks." I laughed. "And practically grabbed your face that one time."

"You were a bit aggressive, yes."

"And you were so sweet," I said to him. "You led me to Liv's bed, laid me back, told me to close my eyes, and then kissed me softly."

"And then you shoved your tongue down my throat." He laughed. "And Liv came in and screamed."

"That was hilarious." I giggled. "I can still remember the look of horror on Liv's face when I told her that I'd kissed you and that you were my first kiss. She looked like she wanted to throw up."

"She never let me forget about it." He grinned and then pulled into a parking spot. "I think that was part of the reason I didn't bring up us having slept together with you. I didn't know how you felt, and I didn't want there to be any awkwardness in your relationship with Liv."

"Oh, Aiden." I sighed. "I thought you hated me. I thought you thought I was some sort of crazy slut or something and you were embarrassed."

"Never." He shook his head and turned off the engine and faced me. "You know I've always been attracted to you."

"You have?" I asked, my eyes wide.

"Hasn't that been obvious the last couple of months?" He grinned. "I can't keep my eyes off of you."

"Well, you have kept your hands off of me," I said and realized he'd said eyes and not hands. "Oops, I mean eyes."

"I've had a hard time keeping both off of you." He looked directly into my eyes. "I think us all getting together for Gabby's fake engagement, and then with Xander and Liv has really made me see what I've been missing."

"Yeah, we have been around each other a lot recently," I said with a small smile. "I've had a hard time keeping my eyes off of you as well."

"Well, I am super handsome." He gave me a smug smile, and I hit him in the shoulder.

"And modest as well."

"Always modest." He grinned. "Shall we go in and eat?"

"Yes, please. I'm hungry hungry."

"Well that's not good. We can't have you hungry hungry."

"Oh, why not?"

"Because that will make you too weak for tonight."

"What's happening tonight?" I asked him, my heart racing.

"You'll just have to wait and see." He grinned and I watched as he got out of the car. I unbuckled my seatbelt and looked into my handbag and smiled at my handcuffs. I was pretty certain I was going to check that last box tonight as well. I was going to see Aiden on the bed and both of us would be wearing nothing but our smiles.

NINE

*How do you tell your best
friend's brother that you want
him to dominate you?*

"WOULD YOU LIKE TO HAVE a glass of wine?" Aiden asked me as soon as I sat down on his couch.

"Yes, please," I said, more because I wanted to check out his living room without me looking nosey than actually wanting some more wine.

"White or red?"

"Surprise me," I said and slipped my heels off of my feet. I let out a huge sigh of relaxation as my toes sprang free from their confines.

"You okay?" Aiden took a step towards me and looked down at my feet.

"The heels were killing me." I smiled and rubbed my toes and Aiden took another step towards me.

"Why did you wear them, then?"

"Did you see the look on the faces of all the men when I walked into the restaurant?" I grinned up at him. "Those looks are worth a little pain."

"What about the look on my face when I saw you in those killer heels?"

"What look?" I asked softly as he dropped to his knees in front of me. I thought I was about to have a heart attack. What was he going to do next? A million different scenarios went through my head. For some reason, I kept picturing him pushing the skirt of my dress up, pulling my panties down, opening my legs and burying his head next to my womanhood and darting his tongue inside of me. I shifted on the seat slightly as I was starting to feel very excited.

"This one." Aiden's face came closer to mine, and I gasped as I saw the pure desire shining through his eyes. He reached down and grabbed my right foot and started to massage it and a jolt of lust danced around my body.

"What are you doing?" I moaned, unable to stop myself from trying to wiggle away from him.

"Making your toes all better," he said in a deep voice as he dropped my right foot and then started massaging my left foot. "I can't have you in any pain."

"Oh no?"

"No." He shook his head and bent his mouth so that he was kissing my toes. I have to admit that I was sitting on the edge of my seat. This was even more exciting than I'd anticipated. And then he took my big toe in his mouth and starting sucking on it and my panties immediately grew wet. I could feel an ache in my pussy as he sucked every single one of my toes, his eyes never leaving mine. The feelings of desire in my body had multiplied, and I felt like my body was made of jelly. "Are you feeling better now?" he said with a smug smile and stood up.

"Uh, yeah." I nodded. "Now about that wine?"

"Should you really be drinking?" he asked softly.

"I had a glass of wine at the restaurant."

"Yes, but do you really need a second?"

"Uhm, you offered."

"I just want you to be completely with me tonight."

"I am with you," I said, my voice catching. *Oh, my God, he's going to ask me to be his sub.*

"I'm just teasing." He laughed. "I know you and Liv seem to think I'm a bossy-boots."

"We don't just think. We know. You're very bossy."

"Yet you're still here with me."

"Yes, I am." I nodded. "Now go and get me my wine."

"Now who's bossy?" He laughed, got up and walked away. "Stay there. I'll be right back."

"Okay," I called out and looked around his living room. Aiden's apartment was absolutely huge. He'd moved in a few months ago, and I hadn't realized that it was so luxurious. The floors were a white Carrara marble and warm below my feet as I walked around. There was a huge white shag rug in front of his black leather couch and his coffee table was all glass. There was a large expanse of windows overlooking the city, and I stared at all of the lights and cars before walking over to his massive bookshelves that took up an entire wall on the left of the room.

"See anything you'd like to read?" he asked as he walked back into the room with a bottle of wine and two glasses.

"What do you recommend?" I asked and watched as he placed the bottle and glasses on the table and walked back over to me.

"Anything by Vonnegut," he said and picked up a book called *Slaughterhouse-Five*. "And if you haven't yet read *Fahrenheit 451*, by Ray Bradbury, you're missing out."

"Oh, okay." I looked at the covers and smiled weakly. They didn't look like books I would be interested in reading.

"What do you like to read?" he asked softly as he gazed at my face with a small smile.

"Mainly romance," I said honestly. "I like some contemporary literature as well."

"Romance?" He grinned. "Do you mean books with Fabio covers and lots of swooning women begging to be taken?"

"This isn't the 1980s." I laughed. "Fabio is no longer on the covers, and the women aren't begging for anything." I stared into his eyes and licked my lips slowly. "In the books I read, the women are domineering and taking what they want. In the books I read, the men are begging them to give them a chance."

"So, fiction, then?" He laughed and I shook my head.

"Not necessarily." I turned away from him and looked at his bookshelf. I saw a hardback copy of the *Kama Sutra* and pulled it down. "Nice," I said with a grin as I opened it and stared at pictures of a couple in different sexual positions.

"An ex got it for me," he said with a smile, and I immediately put the book back. A surge of jealousy spread through me at the thought of him and another woman trying out the moves in the book.

"I'm joking, Alice." His hand rubbed my lower back. "Scott bought it for me when I was twenty-one."

"Oh, funny." Suddenly, I felt cheerful again. "What's this?" I picked up a smaller black book with the title *The Marquis De Sade.*

"It's a biography on the Marquis."

"Oh, are you interested in him, then?"

"Do you mean am I interested in sadomasochism?" he asked in a light tone, and I nodded.

"No." He shook his head. "Don't get me wrong, I can do a little candle wax, but that's as far as I'm willing to push it."

"Ooh, okay."

"Bondage and Dominance is another story, though." He winked at me and my jaw dropped as he walked back over to the coffee table and opened the bottle of wine. "Here you go." He handed me a glass of red wine and I took a large gulp as my heart was racing and I wasn't sure I was going to be able to keep my hands off of him for much longer.

"Thank you," I said and watched as he took a small sip of his wine.

"Music?" he asked and walked over to his TV stand and pulled out his phone. "What would you like to listen to?"

"Garth Brooks, please." I smiled at him sweetly, and he laughed.

"Sure," he said, and I looked at him in surprise as he placed his phone on his iPhone dock and the strumming of guitar strings boomed out from his speakers. I felt my body react in shock when I heard Garth's voice crooning into the room as his hit song "Friend's in Low Places" played.

"You actually own a Garth Brooks song?"

"Why, of course." He winked at me and moved closer towards me. "Would you like to dance?"

"To this?" I was shocked once again.

"You don't think I can hoedown?"

"No," I laughed.

"Well, you're wrong." He handed me his glass and started moving back and forth. I watched as he danced to the song, and my jaw dropped as he did a spin around.

"Oh my God, Aiden Taylor, you surprise me every single day." I laughed.

"Put the glasses down." He grabbed them from me and placed them on the table and then grabbed my hands and started moving with me around the room. "I got friends," he sang and looked at me and my heart thudded. And this time, it was not in a sexual way. This time it was the blooming of love in my heart. This time, my heart was racing because the moment was so perfect and Aiden was the perfect man for me.

"Okay, my choice now." He broke away from me and I watched as he walked over to his phone and selected another song. I stood there in anticipation and waited to hear which one he had chosen.

"Sam Cooke?" I said with a smile as the singer's smooth voice crept into the room and caressed our ears. "'Only Sixteen'?"

"Yes." He grabbed my hands again and pulled me towards him so that we were slow dancing. He sang into my ear and we moved along to the music, our bodies pressed into each other. "Only sixteen," he sang along with the song and suddenly I was transported back to when I was sixteen.

"Do you remember when you taught me how to waltz?" I asked him softly and he looked down at me with a grin.

"How could I forget? You almost broke my toes," he teased.

"No, I didn't." I laughed. "You almost broke mine."

"I wasn't sure why you were asking me to teach you how to waltz."

"I wanted to know in case a guy asked me to dance at Homecoming."

"You were sixteen and in high school." He laughed. "No guy was going to ask you to waltz."

"I didn't know that." I laughed. "That was my first dance. I thought it would be like *Dirty Dancing*."

"You must have been disappointed, then." He grinned and swung me back.

"Just a little." I nodded. "But only because Patrick Swayze wasn't there."

"Oh no, how could he stand you up?"

"I don't know," I said and he held me closer to him. "He didn't even get to see the new skills I'd learned."

"Skills I was happy to teach you, by the way."

"You didn't seem happy."

"Oh, I was very happy."

"Really?" I raised an eyebrow at him and he stopped moving and looked at me.

"Oh, I was very, very happy." He grinned. "Almost as happy as I am now."

"Oh? Why is that?" I asked and moaned slightly as he brought me into him even closer. I could feel something hard next to my stomach and I wasn't sure if it was his belt buckle or something else. Well, if I'm honest, I was pretty sure it was something else. Something just waiting to have some fun with me.

"I'm happier now because we're both adults." He leaned into me as his hands moved down to my ass and cupped my butt cheeks.

"Why is that?" I asked again, moving my face closer to his and closing my eyes. I was so anxious to feel his lips on mine that I moved my arms up and hung them loosely around his neck.

"So I could do this," he said and my eyes popped open as his hands lifted my dress up and ran down my bare ass. "You're wearing a thong."

"You got me." I grinned, and he groaned as I shifted against him.

"Oh, Alice." He grunted and then kissed me hard, his tongue seeking instant entrance into my mouth. The taste of wine on his lips was intoxicating as I kissed him back. My hands reached into his hair, and I tugged at his silky tresses as he continued to squeeze my ass.

"Aiden," I groaned as his hands moved up my body and he stepped back and caressed my breasts.

"You're so beautiful, Alice." He palmed my breasts and then played with my nipples through the thin material of my dress. "So, so beautiful." His voice was husky as he pulled me towards him and just held me for a few seconds.

"Take your dress off," Aiden said and stepped back away from me. My body missed the warmth of his next to mine and I tried to move back towards him. "No." He shook his finger at me. "No touching. Not yet."

"Oh." I pouted.

"Take your dress off."

"What's the magic word?" I asked with a small smile.

"There is no magic word required." He growled and grabbed my wrists and pulled me towards him. "You do what I say, when I say."

"Or what?" I breathed out, my body throbbing in excitement at his aggressive tone.

"Or this." His fingers ran down the side of body and back up again, rubbing the sides of my breasts roughly. He pulled me towards him and carried me towards the tall floor-to-ceiling glass window.

"Put your hands against the window," he growled as he faced me toward the window and stood behind me. I placed my fingers against the glass and stared at all the lights in front of us.

"No one can see us, right?" I asked softly as he reached in front of me and grabbed my breasts.

"I don't know," he said huskily as he hands slid up my arms and held my hands against the window. "Do you care of they can?" he whispered into my ear as he moved up closer behind me. I could feel his hardness against my ass and I closed my eyes and mumbled something incoherently. This had gotten a lot hotter and sexier than even I had anticipated.

"I'm going to have you tonight, Alice." He kissed my neck. "I'm going to have you screaming my name and doing things you never thought you would do."

"What things?"

"Take off your dress first," he growled and stepped away from me. I turned around slowly and looked at him. His eyes were dark with desire, and I could see a nerve throbbing in his throat. His tie was slightly undone and he looked like the sexiest unkempt man I'd ever had the pleasure of seeing. I stood in front of him silently and slowly pulled my dress off and threw it at his chest.

I heard his loud intake of breath as he stared at my almost naked body. I was wearing a red thong and red lace bra to match my red heels. I knew that he could see my nipples pointing out because my bra was practically see-through.

"Take off your panties," Aiden said and I have to admit I was slightly taken aback. Turned on as hell, but taken aback, definitely.

"Take my panties off?" I asked breathlessly.

"Yes. Now," he said and placed his hand out.

"Uhm, what?" I said and shivered slightly.

"Take. Your. Panties. Off. Now. *Por favor.*" He didn't smile as he stared at me.

"I thought you didn't know Spanish?" I joked, but he didn't respond. I took a deep breath and pulled my thong down and stepped out of it quickly and handed it to him.

"*Gracias*," he said and winked at me. His gaze narrowed and he stared down at my womanhood with a small smile. "I like the landing strip," he said with a smirk.

"Hopefully you can land in the right place."

"Have no fear. I'm a good pilot," he said, and then he did something I've never seen happen in anything other than a porno. He put my panties to his nose and breathed them in, and he closed his eyes and made a noise before opening them again and looking at me. "You smell good enough to eat."

"That's good to know." I swallowed hard and licked my lips nervously.

"In fact, I think I'm hungry now," he said and stuffed my panties in his pocket. "Take your bra off."

"What does my bra have to do with your hunger?" I said and gasped as he took a step towards me and slid my right strap down my arm. "I thought you wanted me to take it off?"

"I can't wait," he growled and unclasped my bra and then threw it to the ground. He looked down at my naked breasts and leaned down and sucked on my right nipple while playing with my left breast. I moaned as his teeth tugged on my nipple and he seemed to enjoy the sound, as his sucking became even more teasing.

"Oh, Alice," he groaned and fell to his knees. "Come here." He grabbed my waist and pulled me forward so that my sex was mere inches from his face.

"What are you doing?" I gasped, my pussy trembling as I felt the cool air between my legs.

"You," he growled and pulled me forward so that his face was directly in between my legs. "Lean back against the window," he said as he pulled back slightly. I did as he said and leaned back against the cold window. I wondered if anyone could see us and if they could, what they were thinking. They'd be seeing my naked back, and ass and my trembling body.

"Oooh," I cried out as I felt his tongue licking me. "Aiden!" I screamed as I felt him sucking on my clit.

"Shhh," he mumbled against me and his hands pushed my legs apart again. His tongue continued to lick me and I could feel my legs buckling around his face as he continued to pleasure me. I couldn't believe how great it felt. I couldn't wait to tell Liv. Couldn't wait until she heard that there was a new Mr. Tongue in town. Oh God, but was Aiden a master with his tongue or what? I could barely control my screams as his tongue slid inside of me and moved in and out. His tongue was so thick that it felt like a cock, and my body was moving back and forth in time to his movements. And then he held my hips still and just gyrated my wetness on top of his face.

"Aiden, I can't ..." I mumbled as I felt my clit rubbing against different parts of his face. It was the most exciting and sexy thing I'd ever done, and I couldn't quite believe that it was happening. And then he stopped moving my hips and his tongue entered me again, furiously and like a hurricane, and I came within seconds. My orgasm didn't make Aiden slow down though— no, if anything it charged him up even more and his tongue went into double-time pleasuring me and licking up my juices. My body felt spent by the time he finally stood up and I put my arms around him.

"Full now?" I whispered, my eyes shining into his.

"Not even close." He shook his head, and I laughed. I reached up to his tie and undid it and threw it to the ground. Then I started undoing his shirt, my fingers grazing against his chest as I pulled his shirt off and threw it next to his tie.

"Now my pants," he said with a challenge, and I grinned at him. I undid his belt buckle and slid his belt off. Then I undid his pants, reached in and pulled out his very hard erection. He groaned as my fingers moved up and down his cock quickly, excited to bring him the same pleasure as he'd given me. He closed his eyes as I played with his cock and then I dropped to my knees and took him into my mouth eagerly. His cock tasted salty as it slid against my tongue, and I sucked on it fervently as if it were a juicy lollipop.

"Don't stop, Alice," he groaned as he surrendered completely to my blowjob. I grinned to myself as I sucked on the tip of his cock; his precum tasted warm and briny, and he groaned as I sucked him dry. And then I pulled away, and he swore as I stood up.

"What are you doing?" he groaned as he pulled me towards him.

"Waiting for the magic word," I said with a smile and then he laughed out loud.

"I'll give you the magic word, all right." He growled and turned me around so that I was facing the window again. He put his arms around my waist and pulled my ass back so that I was leaning forward.

"Aiden," I said uncertainly and then froze as I felt the tip of his cock running up and down between my legs. "Oh, oh, oh!" I cried out as he brushed my very wet entrance.

"What's the magic word, Alice?" he said and I felt him fumbling in his pocket. His hand moved from my waist for a second and I heard him ripping a packet open. I looked to the ground and saw that it was a condom wrapper. Aiden slid it onto his hardness and then rubbed it directly against me again.

"Oooh, please!" I cried out as the tip of it entered me slowly. I just wanted him to fuck me. Oh so badly. I needed to feel him inside of me.

"Oh, please?" he said and laughed as he slid into me slowly and then pulled all the way out. My whole body was shaking as I felt his fingers rubbing my clit gently and then with more urgency.

"Aiden, please, just, oooh!" I screamed as his fingers moved even faster and then his cock entered me deeply and roughly. "Aiden!" I screamed out and then he grabbed both of my hips and moved in and out of me quickly. My breasts were pushed up against the glass, and I almost felt like I was having an out-of-body experience. The pleasure was too great, too extreme, and too perfect. I felt like I was going to burst. His fingers kept up their movement on my clit as his cock filled me up and I knew that I was close to the biggest orgasm of my life.

"Come for me, Alice," he grunted as he increased his pace.

"I'm about to!" I screamed and seconds later, my body was shuddering with my orgasm. It was then that I felt Aiden push into me a few more times and then he stilled as he exploded inside of me. He then pulled out of me and turned me around and kissed me passionately.

"Let's go to my room now."

"You're still hungry?" I asked and yawned slightly as he kissed my cheek.

"I'm always hungry for you." He chewed on my lower lip. "And I haven't finished with you for the night."

"Oh, you haven't?" I laughed, feeling giddy.

"Oh no." He picked me up and carried me to the bedroom. "Not by a long shot."

"Promise?" I giggled as he plopped me down onto his bed.

"That's a promise I can keep." He leaned down and kissed me hard. "Stay there. I'm going to get us some water."

"Okay," I said as I snuggled into his sheets.

"Don't fall asleep." He laughed as he hurried out of his room. I lay there with a huge smile on my face and a satiated feeling of happiness filling me.

THE NEXT MORNING I WOKE up to Aiden kissing my neck and I smiled as I stretched alongside him.

"Morning, beautiful," he said and gave me a quick kiss. "I'm going to make us some breakfast, okay?"

"Okay." I nodded shyly and smiled at him. "Then I should leave. I need to go to work. I need to work on some listings for some of the realtors today."

"Aww, I was hoping we could have a lazy day in bed." He made a face and sucked on my shoulder. "You sure I can't change your mind?"

"Haha, I wish I could stay." I ran my fingers down his back. "But unfortunately work calls today."

"Pity." He jumped out of the bed and walked to the door. "Stay there. I want to bring you breakfast in bed," he said and then left the room. I lay there with a grin on my face and I was debating calling in sick when I heard Aiden's phone beeping on the side table and while I knew I should ignore it, I couldn't stop myself from picking it up. And this time I wasn't trying to be nosey. This time I didn't have any suspicions or fears. This time I did it just to do it. And then I saw the text on the screen. I dropped the phone back down onto the side-table and got under the sheets and closed my eyes. All I could see was the text on Aiden's phone from Elizabeth. The text that had sucker punched me. The text that had read, "So she asked about the cuff marks??" I was gobsmacked by the comment. What was going on here and what exactly was the relationship between Aiden and Elizabeth?

I ATE BREAKFAST QUICKLY, AND it took everything in me not to ask Aiden what the hell he was playing at with Elizabeth and myself, but I wanted to speak to Liv first. I needed her to tell me what she thought I should do. I was in a precarious situation because I really wanted to be with Aiden, but I also didn't know what I could demand from him, if we weren't really together like that. I needed to think everything through and decide what my next plan of action was going to be because I knew I just couldn't keep on like I'd been doing anymore. I wanted some answers and I wanted the truth.

TEN

Bling bling says the ring

I KNEW AS SOON AS I walked into the apartment after work that something was off. The air felt chilly and the rooms were too quiet. I closed the door quietly and stood there for a few seconds wondering why I felt as if I were out-of-place in my own home.

"Alice, is that you?" Liv cried out my name and I followed the sound of her voice to the kitchen.

"Of course it's me. Who else would it be?" I asked with a small laugh, though my insides were tense. "What's going on?" I asked with a small frown as Liv was sitting at the kitchen table with a teapot and two cups in front of her.

"Want some tea?" she asked brightly, and I couldn't stop from making a face.

"No, I don't want some tea. We never drink tea." I sat down across from her. "We only got that tea set in case we met some hot English guys, so we could invite them back for tea and biscuits."

"True." She smiled. "That never happened, though."

"Yeah," I sighed. "Who knew that all British guys weren't hot?"

"Or into tea." She laughed. "They preferred beers."

"Or pints, as they called them." I grinned. "And lagers."

"Oh yeah, what was that one lager called?" Liv made a face. "Fosters?"

"Oh yeah, that was gross." I giggled and then sat back and stared at her face. "What's going on?" I asked again, my heart racing as the room went still and quiet. Was Liv about to tell me that Aiden and Elizabeth were dating and that he had played me the previous night? I'd been so nervous all day, and I'd been upset that I hadn't asked him exactly what was going on with the two of them. A part of me was scared that he was going to say something that I didn't want to hear. Liv looked uncomfortable as she stared at me and I could tell that she was nervous. "Liv," I asked softly and then I gasped. "Is Aiden dating Elizabeth?"

"Huh?" She looked at me in confusion. "What are you talking about?"

"Is Aiden with Elizabeth?"

"Wait, what?" She frowned. "Didn't you spend the night with Aiden? Didn't you text me that you were staying over?"

"Yes, I did."

"So why do you still think he's with Elizabeth?"

"Long story." I sighed. And watched as she twirled with her hair. My heart dropped as I looked at her. "You don't have cancer, do you?"

"What?" Liv looked confused. "No, no, of course not."

"Then what's going on?"

"Xander proposed to me last night." She bit her lower lip and just stared at me for a second. I stared back at her in shock as she looked at me uncertainly. I have to be honest here; I felt two emotions at her words. The first emotion I felt was extreme happiness for her and when I say extreme happiness, I mean I immediately started grinning in excitement. But, if I'm honest, my smile hid my other emotion. And that was fear. Fear that emanated from my disappointment, jealousy, worry and anxiety. In that moment, I wanted to burst into tears. There were too many things going on, too many things changing, too many uncertainties in my life and I could barely stay afloat.

"Oh my God, let me see the ring!" I said finally and grabbed her hand and gasped out loud. "Whoa," I said, impressed, as I stared at the gigantic rock on her finger. "Did he go to South Africa and mine that himself?" I said, my eyes wide. "That's huge."

"Isn't it?" she said, her eyes equally wide. "I think it's too big."

"There is no such thing as too big." I laughed and then paused. "I thought he was going to give you his family ring though?"

"I think that he felt bad about proposing with that ring after Gabby had worn it." Liv made a face, and I groaned. Sometimes I forgot that Xander had been in a fake engagement with Liv's older sister, Gabby.

"As he should," I said and then looked at her ring again and squealed. "Oh my God, Liv, I'm so excited for you."

"You're not upset?" she asked hesitantly.

"Of course I'm not upset." I shook my head at her. "I'm so happy for you. Okay, I admit I'm a little jealous, but you know I'm so happy for you."

"It's going to be so weird," she said with a sigh.

"What is?"

"Leaving here. Leaving you. Moving in with, Xander."

"When are you leaving?" I asked nonchalantly, my stomach in knots. I was going to be alone at twenty-two. I had known she was planning on moving out anyways, but now it all seemed so real.

"Not until we're married," she said with a smile. "I told Xander I don't want to live together until we're married."

"Oh." I bit my lower lip and paused for a second without speaking. "Isn't it a bit late to be taking a virginal stance?" I squeaked out. "Didn't you already tell him you were going to move in with him?

"Virginal stance?" She grinned. "What are you talking about?"

"You not living with Xander before you're married."

"I'm not doing that because I don't want to live in sin." She laughed. "I'm doing it for you."

"For me?"

"Yes!" She shook her head. "I know you don't want me to move out, and I don't want to either. I'd love for Xander to move in and we all live together, but he would never go for that. And remember he kinda already asked me to move in with him, and I kinda already said yes."

"What?" My jaw dropped. "You don't have to do this for me. If you want to live with him beforehand, you should."

"He asked me to move in before he proposed and while I was happy, I didn't really know what to say," she said with a shy smile. "I didn't know how to tell you then and I felt so bad how you found out, but I thought about it and I don't want to move out and leave you just yet. So I told him I prefer that we don't move in together until we're married."

"Wow." I felt as if I were in shock. "I don't know what to say."

"Neither did he." She laughed. "I don't think he was too happy that I changed my mind about moving in earlier."

"Dump him, then." I laughed. "Find a guy who will be cool with that situation. Who needs Xander anyway? Tell him to keep his cheap-ass ring," I joked, and Liv laughed.

"You know how much I love him," she said dreamily, and I nodded as we both gazed at her beauty of a ring.

"I know."

"This is it for me, Alice." Her eyes were soft as she gazed at me. "He's the one I've been waiting for my whole life. He's the one who makes me feel whole. He's my better half. My perfect half. And he loves me. He really loves me. After everything." She stopped then and grabbed my hands. "I never thought I'd meet someone like him."

"I know. And you deserve him," I said seriously. "He's perfect for you. I'm so happy for you, Liv."

"I want you to have what I have." She squeezed my hands. "I want you to be loved and to love like I love."

"Maybe it's just not in the cards for me," I said, my eyes watering. "Maybe I'm not the girl who gets the forever love. Maybe I'm not the girl who gets the guy. Maybe I'm just destined to be by myself forever." A lone tear fell from my eyes, and I looked down and I felt my heart breaking for the millionth time that week "Maybe I'm that girl who gets no one."

"You've got Aiden."

"I don't know what I've got with Aiden," I groaned and more tears fell from my eyes. "We spent last night together and it was wonderful, Liv. It was so perfect, and I felt as if my heart and soul were on fire. He was perfect. The perfect lover."

"Ugh," Liv groaned. "This is weird to hear about my brother."

"I'm sorry."

"It's fine." She smiled. "I can deal with it."

"He did things to me, Liv." My voice dropped. "You don't even want to know, but he bossed me around and made me strip off and then we made love against his window."

"His window?" Her eyes widened.

"You had to be there." I laughed. "Let's just say it was hotter than hot."

"Wow."

"But then Elizabeth texted him." I bit my lower lip.

"And said what?"

"She asked him something about me seeing the handcuff marks."

"No way!" Liv's mouth dropped open. "Why would she ask him that?"

"I don't know." I shook my head. "I was too scared to ask him." I sighed. "Do you think he is seeing both of us? Do you think I should pretend to have another boyfriend to try and make him jealous?"

"No." Liv shook her head vehemently. "Maybe we've gone about this the wrong way," Liv said after a few seconds.

"What do you mean?" I looked up at her and wiped my tears from my eyes.

"Maybe we've been too immature." She sighed. "Maybe we tried playing too many games."

"You think so?"

"I think so." She nodded. "And so does Xander."

"Huh?" I sighed. "What did he say?"

"He said that he thinks we need to grow up."

"What?" My jaw dropped.

"I know, right?" Liv wrinkled her nose. "I was like, excuse me, who do you think you're talking to?" Then she paused. "But I think he's right. Maybe all the games and tricks and stuff aren't the way to go about getting a guy."

"It worked for you," I said softly.

"Barely," she said. "And maybe the games didn't help me. Maybe it was the games that nearly made me lose him."

"Yeah," I sighed. "I guess we're really growing up now."

"Yeah." She nodded. "Who would have thunk it?"

"A skunk." I grinned at her and blew my nose. "A skunk would have thunk it."

"I love you, Alice." She squeezed my hand. "My brother's an idiot if he can't see how perfect you are for him."

"We both already know he's an idiot."

"That is true." She grinned. "Hey, before I forget, will you be my maid of honor?"

"Try and stop me." I laughed.

"I have some advice for you." She wrinkled her nose. "Well, the advice comes from Xander, but it's good advice."

"What's the advice?"

"Xander thinks you need to have a serious talk with Aiden. He thinks you need to tell him everything you're thinking and see where he stands."

"I don't know about that." I made a face. "I don't want him to think I'm a sad case."

"You should have a conversation with him," she said and then grinned. "I just had an idea."

"Oh, gosh, what idea?" My eyes narrowed. "Didn't we say that we need to be mature from here on out?"

"We do." She held up her finger. "Hold on, let me get something." She jumped up, ran out of the room and returned a minute later with her laptop. "You need to go here."

"Where?" I looked at the page on her screen. The site said "Kat's Corner" and had a pair of furry handcuffs on the top of the screen. "What's Kat's Corner?"

"That's where you're going to take Aiden."

"I'm going to take Aiden to Kat's Corner? Why?"

"Because you want to show him that you can be all things." She grinned. "Imagine how shocked he'll be if you bring up the BDSM stuff first; unless of course you guys discussed it last night."

"Well, we didn't discuss it." I grinned. "But I think it was pretty obvious that he was into taking control."

"Text him," Liv said. "Text him and tell him to meet you there tomorrow night."

"What?" My eyes widened. "You're being serious?"

"Totally serious." She nodded. "Put all your cards on the table and let's see what he says."

"You think this is a good idea?"

"Oh yeah." She nodded. "My brother needs to stop playing games. Put it all on the table, and let's see how he reacts."

"Okay." I grinned back, even though I was really nervous. "Here goes." I grabbed my phone and texted Aiden. "Here's to special BDSM stores and the truth."

"Here's to you and Aiden," Liv said and jumped up. "Now we need to drink some champagne and celebrate the fact that Xander wants to marry me."

"Here's to Xander and you getting married, and here's to me getting a good spanking from Aiden." I giggled. "Or maybe here's to Aiden getting a good spanking from me."

ELEVEN

Oops! I did it again

WHAT I KNOW ABOUT A Dom/sub relationship is virtually nothing aside from what I've read in two erotic romance books and seen in one almost-porn movie. Needless to say, that doesn't make me an expert or even close to an expert. That was why I'd decided to rent a room at Kat's Corner, a local sex store and club that specialized in introducing couples to dominatrix relationships. You could rent rooms with all sorts of equipment, outfits and toys for a couple hundred dollars, and I had taken money out of my Louis Vuitton handbag fund to rent the room. I wanted to show Aiden that I was the sort of girl who enjoyed spice and that I was the girl to enjoy his alternative lifestyle. At least that's what the lady at the front of the store had said when I'd rented the room. She'd said that alternative lifestyles were for men and women who enjoyed spice and didn't mind straying from the norm. I nodded and smiled as if I knew exactly what she was talking about. I didn't really know what I was willing to do and accept. It was all a pretty new process to me and the more I thought about it, the more I was worried that

I wasn't the sort of person who could feel relaxed doing heavens knows what. Even though the other night with Aiden had been hot.

I was also surprised that Aiden was into this stuff as well. I just didn't see him as being completely Dominant, but what did I know? He'd told Xander, and Xander had told me, and now I was going to show him—well, hoping to show him—that I could be the ball to his chain. Or maybe it was the chain to his ball. Or maybe it was the tongue to his balls. Or the tongue on his balls. I giggled as I groaned at myself. This relationship was never going to make it off the ground if I couldn't stop myself from making stupid jokes.

Knock. Knock. My breath froze as I realized Aiden was here. It was time for me to go into action. I took a quick breath and shook my hands out to calm my nerves before he came into the room.

"Can I come in?" Aiden's voice sounded confused through the door and I knew that he was wondering where he was. The sign on the outside of the store said "Kat's Corner" and so it wasn't completely evident that this was a sex store, or in fact that this was a BDSM store. Unless, of course, he'd been here before, and I didn't want to think about that possibility.

"Hold on," I said and checked my appearance one last time in the mirror and fluffed my hair. I licked my lips and walked towards the door and opened it slowly. Aiden was standing there with a confused look on his face and his eyes widened as he took in my appearance. I was in a short plaid skirt and a white halter-top. I was going for the naughty schoolgirl look, a la Britney Spears' music video, "Oops! I Did it Again," as I'd read that was a favorite fantasy of most men, and I wanted to do everything I could to turn Aiden on.

"Alice?" he said hesitantly, still standing on the other side of the door.

"Yes, Sir," I said in a breathless voice, getting into my role.

"Sir?" He peered into my eyes curiously, and I grabbed his arm and pulled him into the room.

"Has Sir come to teach me a lesson?" I pouted and pushed my chest out. It was getting harder and harder to keep a straight face and not feel self-conscious as he kept standing there looking like he was in the *Twilight Zone*. This was not how I'd imagined this going down.

"Teach you a lesson?" He raised an eyebrow and then looked around the room. I could see his eyes narrowing as he took in the big king size bed and different toys. He looked back at me with a question in his eyes, and I licked my lips slowly and played with my hair.

"I've been a naughty girl, Sir." I waited for him to respond, my heart racing as I waited on his response. Was this going to be the worst seduction ever?

"You've been a naughty girl?" He pursed his lips and then licked them. "You know what happens to naughty girls, right?"

"No, what happens to naughty girls?" My breath caught and my heart was racing even faster as I realized that he was playing along.

"They get punished," he said with a growl and grabbed me around my waist. "Do you want to be punished, Alice?"

"How are you going to punish me?" I asked and batted my lashes.

"Didn't you forget something?" He growled again as his hands slid down the back of my skirt and he realized that I had no underwear on; not even a thong.

"Oh?"

"Don't forget to call me Sir." He slapped my ass lightly, and my eyes widened.

"Yes, Sir," I purred up at him, feeling exhilarated. This role-playing thing was a lot more exciting than I'd anticipated it being. This was something I could really see myself getting into.

"Forget again, and I'll have to have you perform a special task for me."

"What special task?" I whispered as his mouth came dangerously close to mine. "I mean, what special task, Sir?" I breathed out as his eyes narrowed.

"Nice catch." He grinned at me. "You'd be kneeling in front of me if you hadn't remembered quickly."

"Kneeling in front of you?" I asked with a raised eyebrow.

"Yeah, you'd be on your knees, my zipper would be undone, and my cock would be in your mouth."

"Oh." I swallowed hard. He'd gotten to the kinky shit pretty fast and that delighted me. "That doesn't sound like a punishment, Sir."

"It's not a punishment." He winked at me. "It's a treat before the punishment."

"I ..." My voice trailed off as I could see that he was starting to laugh. What was going on here? Was Aiden really playing along? Was this actually going to work?

"What do you want the punishment to be, Alice?" he whispered into my ear. I could feel the tip of his tongue inside it. "Do you want me to show you what I want to do, or is this just a game to you?"

"It's not just a game. I am enjoying this. I want you to continue." I whispered back, my fingers gripping his shoulders. All pretenses were gone from my voice. This was no longer an act, and I was no longer worried or scared about what was going to happen next.

"Then let us proceed. Sir is ready to start class. I want you to go and lie face down on the bed." Aiden closed and locked the door behind him as he watched me walking to the bed. "You've been a bad, bad girl, Alice."

"Why, Sir?"

"Coming to my class with no underwear." He shook his head. "And then playing with yourself so that you could turn me on."

"I only did that because I thought that was what you wanted," I said breathlessly, excited that he was getting into his role.

"My role was to teach you math." He growled as he walked over to the bed. "It wasn't to teach you how to play with yourself." He lifted up my skirt and slapped my ass. "That's for being a tease."

"Oh, Sir." I moaned as his fingers slipped in between my legs and touched my wetness and then spanked me again lightly.

"And that's for being wet."

"I can't help it if you make me wet, Sir," I murmured and watched as he sat on the bed and lifted my legs into his lap from the mattress.

"Only naughty girls get wet for their teachers," he said as he rubbed my ass. "Only bad girls want their teachers to play with them."

"I am a bad girl," I moaned as he gently rubbed my clit. "I'm a very bad girl."

"Show me how bad you are, Alice." His voice was deep as he lifted me off his lap and put me down on the bed. I have to admit that I was a bit sad that the spanking had stopped already.

"What do you want me to do?" I asked in a silky voice and spread my legs for him. His eyes widened and he gave me a satisfied smile.

"I want you to play with yourself until I tell you to stop." He licked his lips, and I stared back at the challenge in his eyes. Was he serious? "What are you waiting on, Alice?"

"Nothing." I took a deep breath and lowered my right hand in between my legs. As soon as I felt my wetness, I closed my eyes.

"Stop." Aiden's voice was brusque. "Open your eyes, Alice." I opened my eyes and looked up at him, shivering as I saw the intensity in his gaze. "I want you to look at me as you play with yourself. I want to see the pleasure in your eyes as you bring yourself to the brink. I want to experience every emotion you feel as I gaze into your soul." His hand found mine and moved it back and forth across my sex. "I want to see what you do to please yourself, so I know what you like."

"You already know what I like." I gasped as he slipped a finger inside of me.

"Aiden knows what you like. The teacher doesn't." He withdrew his finger and sucked on it. "Now look at me and show me."

"Yes, Sir," I said breathlessly, feeling very much like the naughty girl he'd called me a few minutes before as I reached back down between my legs. I moved my fingers gently, and I stared up into Aiden's blue eyes as I played with myself. I could feel myself getting more and more excited and then his hand grabbed mine and moved it away.

"Now, it's time for teacher to show you how to do it." He grinned and pulled his tie off and rolled over on the bed next to me.

"What are you going to do?"

"Put your hands above your head and hold your wrists together," he said and I felt him tying my wrists together with his tie. "Good. Now you can't touch yourself." He grinned down at me. "Are you going to be a good girl now?"

"Yes, Sir."

"Good." He jumped off of the bed, and I watched as he took his shirt and pants off. He stood there in his briefs for a few seconds and then pulled them off. "I didn't even know this place existed," he said as he climbed onto the bed. "How did you know about it?"

I stared up at him silently for a few seconds. I knew now was not the time to tell him that his sister had found the place for me. That would totally ruin the mood.

"That's for me to know," I said finally, and he growled.

"So you still want to be a bad girl?" He raised an eyebrow at me and his fingers trailed down the valley between my breasts and all the way down my stomach. He then ran his fingertips down my legs, and then I felt his tongue licking back up my legs and my inner thighs. My whole body trembled in sweet anticipation as I felt his breath close to my sex. I moaned as I felt the tip of his tongue next to my clit, and I cried out as he kissed back up my body.

"No," I moaned. "I don't want to be a bad girl."

"That doesn't sound too convincing," he said and jumped off of the bed. "Hmm, let's see what toys we have here." He walked around the room and immediately picked up a flogger and held it up to me. "Shall we use this?"

"If you want." I looked over at him and he licked his lips slowly.

"Or we can use the paddle?" He picked one up and hit it against his hand lightly. "Would you prefer me to use this?"

"I'd prefer your hand," I said shyly, and he smiled.

"You like it when I spank you, don't you?"

"Perhaps, Sir," I said with a smile.

"You're a dirty girl, aren't you? You like it when I put you across my lap. You like it when my big manly hand slaps your juicy butt. You love it when my fingers slid into your wetness. You love it when I rub you. It turns you on, doesn't it?" He was breathing harder, and I watched as he put the flogger and paddle down and grabbed something else from the floor. It looked like a huge feather and he walked towards me with a grin. "I'm going to use this tickler on you."

"No," I groaned. "You know I'm too ticklish."

"That's why I'm going to use it." He chuckled. "I'm going to take you to the edge."

"Then what?"

"Then you're going to beg me to come down." He grinned. "You're going to beg to jump off of the edge."

"I don't like jumping."

"I'll be there to catch you." He ran the feather across my lips and then down my neck and towards my nipples. I writhed on the bed as the feather tickled my nipples, and I groaned as he continued his teasing.

"Aiden, please," I moaned forgetting that I was playing his student.

"Who?" he growled. "My name is Sir."

"Sir, please," I whined as he ran the feather back and forth across my clit.

"Please what?" he said as he stared down at me.

"Please let me come," I groaned. I was so close to coming; yet, he was pushing me to the limits and not finishing the job.

"Not yet." He shook his head. "You can't come until I say so."

"I should have known that you were a control freak," I moaned.

"A control freak?" He laughed. "So now I'm a bossy-boots *and* a control freak."

"Frigging let me come, Aiden!" I moaned as his fingers started rubbing me gently.

"I thought you wanted me to be in charge." He raised an eyebrow. "Isn't this why you invited me to a BDSM club? You want me to dominate you, right?"

"I wanted to know …" My voice trailed off as Aiden slipped two fingers inside of me, and I felt myself orgasm right away. My body shuddered as he moved his fingers in and out of me and then he bent down and licked up my juices with his tongue.

"It looks like teacher is being bad as well." He growled as he positioned his cock at my entrance and rubbed me gently.

"Yes, you are," I groaned and he laughed.

"It's a good thing I like being bad then, isn't it?" He winked at me and then jumped off the bed again. "Hold on, Alice. I'm just getting my rubbers."

"Okay." I tried to move my hands and he laughed.

"Hold on." He climbed back onto the bed and untied my wrists. "So, what do we do next?"

"What do you mean?" I asked him, surprised by his words. "I thought we were about to have sex?"

"Yes, but maybe we shouldn't do it on the bed. Not while we're here at Kat's Corner."

"You're the expert." I licked my lips and ran my fingers down his chest. "What do you suggest we use next?"

"Uhm," he grinned at me and looked around the room, "about that ..." His voice trailed off, and he groaned as I grabbed his hardness.

"About what?" I said, distracted by the fact that he seemed to be growing even harder in my hand.

"Nothing," he said and grabbed my hand and pulled me off of the bed. "Put this on." He grabbed a black latex jacket, with two big holes where my breasts would be.

"This looks like a straitjacket." I frowned as I saw the arms tied together.

"Yes it does. Put it on." He watched me putting it on and stared at my naked breasts. "Why does this look even sexier than when you were naked?"

"I don't want to wear this." I pouted. "I want to be able to touch you."

"It's not about what you want. Not right now." He leaned forward and pinched my nipples.

"You love taking charge, don't you?"

"Of you, yes." He nodded and then grabbed me. "Bend over," he growled as he pushed me forward onto the bed, my ass tilted up as he came in behind me. "I like to know that you're always up for whatever I want," he muttered as he pushed himself into me. "Oh, yes!" he groaned as he moved in and out of me and held onto my hips. I could feel his cock sliding in and out of me quickly, and it felt so weird not being able to move my hands or arms. My breasts brushed against the sheet, and I knew when he was about to come because he paused right before his body shuddered against mine. He then pulled out of me, pushed me down onto the bed and kissed me.

"Oh, Alice." He stroked my face as he panted. "That was fucking fantastic."

"I'm glad I pleased you, Sir." I smiled up at him. "So what shall we do next?"

"Let's talk," he said and kissed me on the lips. "I think we need to talk."

"Okay." I nodded. "Can you take this jacket off me first?"

"Of course," he said with a smile and undid the straps and I pulled the jacket off quickly. "So I need to tell you something."

"Is it about you and Elizabeth?" I asked softly, my heart thudding.

"Yes." He nodded and looked nervous.

"What is it, Aiden?" I pulled away from him slightly, scared about what he was going to tell me.

"It's about Elizabeth and me and how we met," he said with a groan and then looked around the room and sighed.

"Are you guys dating? Is she your girlfriend?" I blurted out.

"No, she's not my girlfriend." He grabbed my hands. "This is hard for me, Alice." He groaned and shook his head. "Why is this so hard?"

"Just tell me, Aiden." I stared into his eyes and I could see that he looked worried. "Are you guys in a Dominant and submissive relationship?" I asked him finally, unable to stand the silence any longer. "Just tell me, Aiden. Are you her Dom?"

He shook his head and then took a deep breath before speaking. "It's worse than that, Alice, it's much worse than that."

TWELVE

Who's your Dom?

MY PHONE RANG THEN BECAUSE you know how life goes, you always get interrupted during the most crucial conversations. And because I'm me and totally stupid, I jumped off of the bed and answered the phone.

"Hello?" I said with a hesitant voice because I didn't recognize the number.

"Alice, it's Henry," said a smooth voice.

"Hey, Henry," I said and got back onto the bed with a smile on my face. Aiden lay there staring at me with narrowed eyes and a frown. "Can I help you?"

"Yes, you can." He laughed and then cleared his throat. "I was hoping we could grab a coffee this weekend?"

"You want to grab a coffee with me?" I asked in shock, my voice rising slightly.

"Yes. I figure seeing as I'm Xander's best man and you're Liv's maid of honor, we should get to know each other better."

"I'd love to get to know you better—eek!" I screamed as I felt Aiden slap my bottom.

"Alice, are you okay?" Henry sounded worried.

"Yes, sorry, I uh, I …" My voice trailed off as Aiden's hands came around my waist and pulled me back to him. "Sorry about that, I'm fine." I gasped as Aiden's fingers pinched my nipples.

"Oh, okay." Henry sounded unsure. "So this weekend? What day is better for you?"

"Uhm, I can do Sat—oooh." I moaned as I felt Aiden entering me. I closed my eyes for a few seconds as I felt him moving inside of me. "Henry, can I call you back, please?" I gasped into the phone.

"Sure. Is everything okay, Alice?"

"Yes!" I gasped and hung up. "What are you doing?" I moaned as Aiden flipped me onto my back and got on top of me.

"That was rude of you," he murmured as he lowered his body onto mine.

"What was?" I gasped as he grabbed my hands and entered me slowly.

"Taking a call while we were talking."

"Well, you were basically telling me that you and Elizabeth are—"

"We're nothing, Alice." He grunted as he kissed me hard.

"What do you mean?" I moaned as he continued moving his cock in and out of me slowly.

"Elizabeth and I are nothing." He groaned and pulled out of me and then sat up on the bed. "I'm going to get blue balls." He made a face.

"What do you mean you and Elizabeth are nothing?" I asked with a frown. I completely ignored his blue balls comment. "You're not sleeping with me while you're in a kinky relationship with her?"

"I'm not in a kinky relationship with her." He made a face. "I hired her."

"You what?" My jaw dropped. "She's a prostitute?" I glared at him. "I knew it. I just knew it."

"No, Alice." He grabbed my hands and grinned. "I don't mean she's a prostitute—she's an actress." He made a face. "I know, I know, it was a stupid thing to do."

"Actress?"

"I wanted to teach you a lesson." He sighed. "Maybe it was a mistake."

"Maybe?" I glared at him. "What are you talking about? Why did you want to teach me a lesson?"

"You and Liv are so immature," he said. "After you hired Brock and Jock and pretended that the two of you were dating them, Xander and I figured that you both needed a taste of your own medicine."

"Xander knew about this?" I was in shock. "What?"

"I thought it would be a good idea." He sighed. "Like I said, I wanted to give you a taste of your own medicine."

"My own medicine?"

"Are you going to repeat everything I say?" He grinned.

"I wouldn't be grinning if I were you." I narrowed my eyes at him. "Continue with your story."

"After I saw you kissing Scott, I got really upset, but then I spoke to Scott and Xander, and I realized that perhaps you did like me, after all."

"Well, duh. Hasn't that always been obvious?"

"Not really, Alice." He shook his head. "Not with all the silly games you and my sister play. I really didn't know what to think."

"I don't play silly games." I pouted, and he leaned forward and kissed my lips.

"Yes, you do, Alice." His fingers ran down my cheek. "And for some reason, I decided that I needed to join you at your own game. So I hired Elizabeth." He smiled at me, but I didn't return his look of adoration. "We decided to do some fake Facebook flirting to trap you, then she sent me some fake texts, I talked about some fake dates, invited her to the football game, which was Xander's idea by the way, and waited for you to take the bait."

"I thought you were dating her as well," I growled. "I was so upset and angry and confused and … Argh." I poked him in the chest. "That was a horrible thing to do."

"I just wanted to see if you would be jealous," he said. "And I wanted you to see how stupid and childish it is to fake relationships and stuff to try and make someone jealous."

"Whatever." I looked away from him, still feeling angry, but also feeling overwhelmingly happy. He didn't like Elizabeth! I was over the moon at the truth.

"I'm sorry, Alice," he muttered. "Can you forgive me?"

"Why did you do it, Aiden?" I looked at him and searched his face. "Did you just want to have one over on me?"

"Are you dense, Alice?" He looked at me in shock. "I like you. I have feelings for you. I've had feelings for you for a long time. I had a feeling you felt the same, but I wanted to make sure you were mature enough for a relationship. And I wanted to make sure that this was something you wanted."

"You like me?" I grinned at him.

"I maybe more than like you." He grinned back and kissed me again.

"Maybe?"

"More than maybe," he said with a laugh. "I just don't want to be your best friend's sleazy older brother."

"You're not sleazy—well, not very sleazy." I grinned.

"Not very sleazy?"

"Well, you know." I grinned again. "You are here with me, naked, in a BDSM store."

"Alice, that goes both ways." He laughed. "So, are you sleazy too?"

"Well, I only came here for you." I blushed. "I wanted you to know that I'd be down with trying your alternative lifestyle."

"About that." He made a face, and my stomach turned slightly.

"Oh God, what now?" I asked, worried. "Don't tell me you're a member of a sex club for real?"

"What?" He laughed. "Not at all, Alice. You know you really have an overactive imagination."

"So what is it you need to tell me now?" I poked him in the chest.

"So, I'm kinda not a Dom." He put his hands up. "Don't kill me."

"What do you mean?" I frowned. "Xander told me that ..." My voice trailed off as I realized that I'd been set up. "That was a lie as well?"

"Yeah." Aiden nodded with a rueful smile on his face. "Xander thought it would be funny."

"Funny?"

"Yeah." Aiden laughed. "He thought it would be interesting to see what you thought up."

"So I let you spank me for fun?" I groaned. "And I called you Sir."

"I liked you calling me Sir." He winked. "You can call me that whenever you want."

"Uh huh."

"And I can spank you whenever you want as well." He reached over and played with my breasts. "In fact, we can do whatever experimentation you want."

"Can I get a strap-on and—"

"No." He cut me off right away and laughed. "Anything but that. There is no way in hell you're using a strap-on on me."

"Aww." I laughed. "What other experimentation are you thinking about, then?"

"Well, I wouldn't mind using a pinwheel." He ran his fingernails across my nipples. "And maybe some anal beads."

"Anal beads?" I raised my eyebrows at him and his eyes glittered at me.

"Anal beads and vibrators and anything else we want." He moved back on top of me. "Anything you're comfortable with."

"I think I can be comfortable with a lot of things," I whispered against his lips as he entered me again. I wrapped my legs around his waist, and he groaned as he moved inside of me, his cock seeming to go deeper and deeper with each thrust.

"Good, because I plan on us doing a lot of experimenting." He slammed into me and leaned down and sucked on my nipples. "And who knows, maybe one day I'll even end up being your Dom."

"Or maybe one day I'll end up being yours." I growled and reached up and slapped his ass hard.

THIRTEEN

Text sex or phone sex?

"GET OUT OF TOWN!" LIV looked shocked as I finished telling her about my night with Aiden. "I'm going to kill Xander. I can't believe he was a part of this plan and didn't tell me a thing."

"Crazy, right?" I beamed at her. I was so happy that Aiden and I were finally being honest with each other that I couldn't hide my excitement.

"Uhm, more than crazy." Liz sat on my bed and giggled. "I can't believe that Aiden did this. I knew there was no way in hell that he was a Dom."

"Well, he could be one. Trust me." I shivered. "You should have seen the way he took me over his knee."

"I have to be honest, I'm not sad that I don't have to see that." Liv grinned at me. "Not trying to be mean, but it still freaks me out knowing you two are sleeping together."

"We don't do much sleeping." I laughed and she groaned. "What can I say, but he's dynamite in bed."

"So what happened after he admitted he'd been lying about Elizabeth, which is pretty ingenious in a way?"

"Well, I told him off a bit." I laughed. "And that's when he told me that he made up the BDSM stuff as well."

"Xander is so tricky." She shook her head. "I bet he knew all along that you would tell me right away."

"Yeah, I think that as well. I mean, it just doesn't seem reasonable that he would think I didn't tell you."

"So that means he knew that I knew all along," Liv groaned. "I'm going to get him back for that."

"Oh? How?"

"I'm going to handcuff him to the bed tonight." She grinned. "And then tease him. Let's see how much he likes handcuffs then."

"Oh, Liv!" I laughed.

"He needs to be punished." She grinned again. "And what better way than from a budding Domme wannabe?"

"You don't want to be a Domme, though."

"He doesn't have to know that."

"Oh, Liv, you're so bad."

"I know." She giggled. "I'm a bad, bad girl."

"That's what I said to Aiden last night." I laughed.

"About me?" She looked confused.

"No, about me." I grinned. "We really got into the role-playing. I think I'm going to ask him to rent a policeman's uniform, and I'll be the criminal he's interrogating."

"Uh, okay." Alice laughed.

"And then maybe I'll be an escort and he can be my John and we can meet up at a hotel bar and he can pretend he's picking me up."

"You do know that prostitution is illegal and if someone thinks you guys are for real, you might get arrested?"

"We'll be fine. He's a lawyer." I grinned. "He can get us out of it if that were to happen."

"You're crazy, Alice."

"Well, so is Aiden. And he likes my crazy. Well, some of my crazy, at least."

"So what happens next?" She grinned and her stomach grumbled. "And do you want to go out to dinner?"

"Yes, let's go and get some fried chicken. I've been craving it." I nodded. "Hold on, let me change real quick."

"Okay." She nodded and followed me to my room. "So you and Aiden are official now?"

"No," I said and sighed as I opened my closet door. "He didn't really say anything about us being in a relationship. He didn't ask me to be his girlfriend or his wife."

"Alice, he's not going to propose just because you had sex."

"I know that." I rolled my eyes. "He didn't propose years ago, either. I guess I just hoped he would say something about us being more official, you know."

"I know." She nodded. "It's hard to be sleeping with a guy and not really have anything confirmed."

"Yeah, I feel like a bit of a slut if I'm honest." I took my shirt off and pulled on a navy sweater. "I mean, don't get me wrong, I enjoy the sex with Aiden, but I kinda feel cheap. And I don't know why. I think that if men can have sex when not in a relationship then I should be able to as well, but it just feels wrong."

"I think it's because you want to be in a relationship with him, so you're kinda in limbo right now."

"Yeah." I nodded as I pulled my jeans on. "I guess I just want that official title of girlfriend."

"That's understandable, Alice. I felt the same way with Xander. Well, kinda. I mean the first night was a one-night stand, but after I'd slept with him a few times, I did start to feel like 'is he really into me and is this about more than sex or not?'"

"Yeah," I sighed and sat on the edge of my bed. "I just want to know where this is going."

"Why don't you ask him?"

"You think so? It seems a bit forward, don't you think? I mean, we barely just admitted that we had feelings for each other."

"Yeah, but I think you've both had feelings for each other for a while." She groaned. "Just ask him."

"Maybe." I sighed. "I don't want to scare him away."

"He's Aiden. He doesn't get scared." Liv grinned. "If anything, he's the scary one."

"He's a bossy bear, not a scary one."

"I know, I know." Liv groaned. "He's the bossy bear who likes to tie you up and have his wicked way with you and you love it."

"Don't be jealous." I giggled as we walked out of my room. "I can't help it if my man has a kinky side."

"Oh, I had a question for you," Liv said as we left the apartment and headed to our favorite fried chicken place a few blocks away.

"What?"

"So what happens with Elizabeth now?"

"No idea," I shrugged and then paused. "Though you wanna know something funny? When we were at the coffee shop and I saw Scott and Elizabeth looking at each other, it seemed to me that they had already met."

"Oh, really?" Liv looked at me curiously. "Like, through Aiden?"

"No." I shook my head and thought back to that moment. "It was as if they knew each other better than that. I don't know. Maybe I imagined it, but I swear I thought to myself that they had a really intense stare for a few seconds and then it passed."

"Ooh," Liv murmured. "I wonder how they know each other?"

"Yeah, me too." I grinned at her. "I'm going to see if I can find out."

"Oh, Alice," she groaned as we walked into the restaurant. "Can we eat first and then figure out a plan?"

"Sure," I said as I took a deep breath and smelled the greasy wonderfulness that was fried chicken and French fries. "Let's eat first."

I LAY IN BED FEELING full and happy. I was about to roll over and go to sleep when my phone beeped.

Hey sweet pea. I grinned as I saw the message from Aiden.

Alice: *Hey.*

Aiden: *I missed you today.*

Alice: *Oh wanted to get some spanking in?*

Aiden: *Hmm. I'd use any excuse to touch your ass.*

Alice: *How was work?*

Aiden: *Good. I thought about you all day though. Had a big boner. :)*

Alice: *Aw, how special!* I typed, but inside I frowned. Was this all about sex to Aiden?

Aiden: *What are you wearing right now?*

Alice: *Why?*

Aiden: *I want to picture you.*

Alice: *Okay ...*

Aiden: *So what are you wearing and where are you?*

Alice: *I'm at a costume party and I'm wearing a rat costume.*

Aiden: *Not sexy. :(*

Alice: *Where are you and what are you wearing?*

Aiden: *I'm in bed. Naked and thinking of you.*

Alice: *Oh Aiden, the words I've always wanted to hear.*

Aiden: *I wish you were here.*

Alice: *I'm sure you do.*

Aiden: *Take your clothes off.*

Alice: *At the party?!*

Aiden: *I know you're not at a party.*

Alice: *Okay, stalker.*

Aiden: *Tell me when your clothes are off.*

Alice: *Why?*

Aiden: *Because then we can play.*

Alice: *Play via text?*

Aiden: *Just take your clothes off.*

Alice: *Okay.* I groaned and took off my T-shirt and shorts. *I'm naked.*

Aiden: *Good. Send me a photo.*

Alice: *No.*

Aiden: *No?*

Alice: *Nope. I don't do naked photos.*

Aiden: *Face time with me then?*

Alice: *Perhaps.*

I jumped out of bed and ran to my dresser and quickly applied some lipstick and blush to my face. I grabbed my comb and brushed my hair as well. There was no way I was going to FaceTime with him looking washed out.

Aiden: *Is that a yes?*

Alice: *It was a perhaps.*

Ring ring. I laughed as I saw the video call coming in from Aiden.

"I said perhaps, not yes." I giggled as I answered the call.

"I wanted to see you." His eyes looked into the phone and I could tell he was trying to see if I was naked. "I can't see you properly," he moaned.

"You can't see my face?"

"I can see your beautiful face, but nothing else."

"What do you want to see?"

"Anything!" He laughed. "And everything."

"Let me see you." I slid onto the bed and lay back.

"Fine." He lowered the phone and showed me his cock being held by his right hand.

"Oh, ready for me already, are you?"

"I've been ready for you since this morning when you left to go to work."

"Well, you had to go to work as well."

"Yeah, but I would have skipped for you." He adjusted the camera, and I was looking at his face closely. "Did you have a good day?"

"Yeah, it was fine. Long and boring, but fine. Liv and I had dinner."

"Oh? What did you have?"

"Fried chicken." I laughed as he made a face.

"You girls love fried chicken."

"Do you have a problem with that?"

"Not at all." He grinned. "So I'm assuming you told Liv about Elizabeth and the BDSM stuff?"

"Yup, she was in shock, and she's going to get Xander back."

"He's expecting it." He laughed. "And, I'm sure, looking forward to it."

"You guys are so devious."

"Hey, Pot, it's Kettle calling."

"Funny, not." I rolled my eyes and lay back. I was happy that the conversation had gone to everyday stuff and wasn't just focusing on sex. "So what about you? Did you have a good day?"

"Pretty good. I met Elizabeth for lunch."

"Oh?" My stomach churned with jealousy.

"Yeah, I needed to give her her final payment."

"Oh, okay." I paused. "So hey, do you know if she knew Scott before all this?"

"Scott my brother?" He looked confused.

"Yes, Scott your brother."

"No, why?"

"No reason." I shook my head. I knew that Aiden wouldn't want me to get involved, so I didn't say anything else to him. "So what else did you do today?"

"Aside from thinking about you?"

"Yeah." I nodded.

"Not much. Counted down the hours until I could call you tonight."

"Aww." I smiled into the phone and then blurted out, "What are we?"

"What do you mean?" He frowned.

"Are we officially dating?"

"Is that what you want?" he asked and the camera slipped so I couldn't see his face.

"I want what you want."

"Why don't we talk about it later?" he said in a soft voice. "Right now, my mind is focused on one thing."

"What's that?" I asked softly.

"The quickest way to making you come without touching you."

"I think you already know." I laughed and settled into the bed.

"I know," he groaned. "I want you to touch yourself, Alice, and I want you to put the phone lower so I can see you."

"You're such a dirty boy, Aiden."

"And that's why you love me." He laughed and I froze. Did he know how true his words were? "Okay, I want you to take your finger and rub your clit gently—yes, like that." He groaned as he watched me playing with myself. I closed my eyes as I ran my fingers back and forth and listened to him telling me what to do. I'd never thought that phone sex or even video chat would be particularly sexy, but I'd been wrong. I was so turned on by the sound of his deep voice telling me what to do that I didn't know what to do with myself.

"Now push one of your fingers inside your pussy," he said dirtily, and I moaned at his words. "Oh, I wish I was with you right now." He grunted. "Put the phone back up to your face. I want to see your face."

"You never stop bossing people around, do you?" I moaned as I looked into the phone and he was gazing at me with lust.

"I want to fuck you so badly." He stretched out his arm and I saw his hand moving up and down on his cock quickly. "I wish you were here, sitting on top of me and riding me. I wish I could touch and taste your juices as you come for me. I wish you were here so badly."

"What would you do if I was there?" I whimpered as I rubbed myself faster.

"I'd grab you and pull you up my body and then I'd have you sit on my face and ride my tongue as I licked you to orgasm." He grunted, and I could see his face twisting as he grew close to orgasm. "And then I'd spin you around and I'd lick your ass as well."

"Aiden!" I said in shock as I continued playing with myself.

"Have you ever been licked in the ass?" he groaned, and I shook my head, not knowing what I thought about that possibility. "You'd love it." He looked directly into the camera. "You'd be my dirty, dirty girl and then I'd flip you onto your knees and slam my cock into you doggy-style and we'd both come so hard and fast that we wouldn't know what happened."

"Oooh!" I cried out as my body bucked from my orgasm.

"That's it, Alice!" he grunted as he came as well. "Moan for me, baby, tell me how badly you want me."

"I wish I had your cock right now," I moaned into the phone. "I wish I could feel you inside of me. I wish I could run my fingers down your back as you fill me up."

"Oh fuck, Alice." I watched as his body shuddered in climax. "That was so fucking hot." He smiled into the phone as he lay back. "I wish I could cuddle with you right now."

"Me too," I said and smiled. "I'd love to be in your arms right now."

"Soon," he said and blew me a kiss. "I have a surprise for you, and I can't wait to see you and hold you in my arms."

"Night, Aiden."

"Night, my sweetness. Have dreams about me." He blew me another kiss, and I stared at his face, knowing that I loved this man more and more every day.

FOURTEEN

Stay with me

"I CAN'T BELIEVE YOU BROUGHT me to a Sam Smith concert for my birthday!" I looked at Aiden in surprise. "That's so sweet of you."

"Liv felt bad that she had to miss your birthday, and she thought this would be a nice idea."

"So you brought me here because of Liv?" I asked, feeling disappointed.

"Did I fly you all the way to San Francisco because Liv felt bad?" Aiden asked with a small smile. "What do you think, Alice?"

"I don't know." I bit my lower lip as we walked into the Bill Graham Civic Auditorium.

"No, I didn't do it as a favor." He laughed and grabbed my hand. "Do you want to stand by the stage or sit down?"

"Do we not have assigned seating?" I looked at him with a frown.

"No." He shook his head. "The seating is first come, first serve."

"Oh." I looked around at the crowds, pretending that I was thinking about my decision, but all I was really thinking about was the fact that he was holding my hand. Aiden Taylor was holding my hand. And I wasn't dreaming.

"So?" He looked down at me, his blue eyes sparkling at me.

"Let's sit down." I looked down at my heels. "I'm not sure how long I'll last standing in these things."

"Seats it is, then." He pulled me closer to him as three guys walked past us and stared at me. "Would you like a drink?"

"Yes, please." I nodded. "A glass of red wine, please."

"Sure." We walked over to a makeshift bar and stood in line. "Also, I brought you here because I wanted to make our first official date a memorable one." He looked self-assured, but there was nervousness to his voice.

"So this is a date?" I wasn't sure if my heart could beat any faster.

"Are you okay with that?"

"Am I?" I giggled. "Yes, I'm okay with that." I didn't make the comment that I was glad that we were finally having an official date after having had sex several times. It wasn't like I'm a super old-fashioned type of girl, but it is nice when the dates come before the sex. Especially the almost Dom and sub sex relationships.

"Good." He put his arm around my waist and kissed the side of my face, right next to my ear and below my hairline, though not exactly on my cheek.

"Good," I said as well, though I wasn't sure why. I was too busy floating in the clouds and daydreaming about what this all meant. Did this mean that Aiden wanted an exclusive relationship with me? Did this mean I was his girlfriend? I felt giddy at the thought, but didn't want to push my luck by bringing up too many questions right away. I knew that if there was one thing that annoyed men it was the 'what are we?' questions right at the beginning of a relationship.

"Here's your wine. Let's go find some seats." He handed me a glass, and we walked over to an escalator and rode it up one flight to another level and walked down a hallway and through an entryway. The place was packed. There were thousands of Sam Smith fans milling around looking for the best seats.

"Let's go over there." Aiden pulled me around a corner and I followed behind him as he walked up some steep steps to get to two empty seats. I looked at the ground as I walked up and held onto the railing. I was scared I was going to trip and fall down the stairs. I didn't even want to see how high up we were as I was scared of heights and had a minor case of vertigo.

"Damn it, there's a column in the way." Aiden sighed as we made our way to the seats. "We can't see the stage properly."

"Oh," I said weakly as I looked down. It was true we couldn't really see the stage properly as the column obstructed our vision being in the middle of the stage, but I didn't really want to move again.

"There are some empty seats over there." He pointed to some seats far off in the corner, and I stifled a groan. My feet were already aching in my too-high and too-tight heels, and my calves were also aching from walking up all the stairs. I didn't really feel like walking down a bunch of stairs and then back up more stairs. In fact, it was almost giving me a minor panic attack. It wasn't going to look sweet or sexy if my face was covered in sweat from all the walking.

"Is that cool?" Aiden looked at me, but he had already started walking towards the stairs again, so I knew that he didn't really want an answer. He'd already assumed that it was going to be okay.

"Yeah, sure. We want to see the stage," I joked, though I honestly didn't care. I loved Sam Smith, and I knew I would enjoy hearing him live, but I knew my mind would be on Aiden more than anything else. I was already wondering if he was going to try anything. Would he rub my leg? Would he try to get me to sit in his lap? Would we kiss? I was so excited about the many different possibilities that I couldn't even think. Which was a good thing as thoughts of him were distracting me from the very real pain that I was feeling in my feet. I wasn't sure why I even bothered trying to wear heels for anything longer than two minutes. My feet always ended up killing me and made me want to kill myself. I knew that as a woman I was meant to suck up the pain for the elongated legs that the heels gave me. The sexy killer legs that made men go weak at the knees, but man, it was hard. Part of me didn't think it was worth it. The same part of me that wasn't feeling the thong riding up the back of my ass at the same time. And the same part that felt uncomfortable in the tight bra and corset that was holding my fat in. I wasn't even sure why I was trying to give the illusion of having no extra body fat. Aiden knew the truth; he knew that I had a belly and that my six-pack was hiding away. He knew, and he didn't care. He thought I was sexy as I was.

"So were you surprised?" he asked me as we waited for the opening act to get started.

"Was I surprised you brought me to San Francisco for our first date? Uh, yes." I laughed. "This is the best first date ever. I'm not sure that any other guys will be able to live up to this first date."

"Well, hopefully, no other guys will have that opportunity," he said and turned away. My heart almost burst out of my chest at his words. I was in shock. He'd practically proposed to me. Well, not really, but you know what I mean. I really wanted to text Liv and ask her what she thought of his comment, but I knew that now was not the time.

"Yeah, we'll see," I said casually and he turned back to me with a smirk on his face.

"We'll see, huh?" He tilted his head to the side. "Have some other first dates lined up, do you?"

"Well, Henry wants to take me out for coffee," I said softly, and he laughed.

"Do you want me to put you over my lap right now?" he whispered in my ear. "Because I will, Alice."

"Excuse me?" I squeaked out.

"I will put you over my lap and spank you," he whispered again as he fingers ran up my leg. "I will spank that ass and then rub it and I'll have you so wet that you won't even want to stay for the concert."

"You wish," I said and gasped as he slipped his fingers between my legs. "Aiden, you can't." I shoved his fingers aside. "There are people here."

"I think you might remember that I don't care who sees me." He winked at me. "You could sit on my lap right now and ride me and I wouldn't say no."

"We'd get put in jail for public sex." I shook my head at him.

"Perhaps." He grinned. "Shall we have a go and see what happens?"

"No." I laughed. "I think not."

"What day are you and Henry meeting up?" He changed the subject and looked more serious.

"Not sure, why?"

"Because I'm coming." He stared at me with a no-nonsense expression.

"You don't have to come."

"I know I don't have to come, but I will." He kissed me hard. "I just want to make sure that he knows you're mine."

"I'm not yours. I'm not a possession," I said, but my heart was racing.

"You're my girl," he said softly. "And I want everyone to know."

"Am I now?" I raised an eyebrow at him, but my heart was racing so fast with excitement that I thought it was in the Olympics.

"I hope so," he said softly and took my hand. "Will you be my girlfriend, Alice?"

"I thought you'd never ask." I smiled at him as my heart fluttered, and he pulled me closer to him and gave me a big kiss.

"I want you to stay with me tonight," he said as he pulled away. I groaned as he laughed.

"You think you're so smart, don't you?"

"I'm not the only one who thinks that."

"Aiden." I grabbed his face and kissed him hard. "No, you're not the only one." I gazed up into his eyes. "The only difference is that I don't just think I'm smart, I know I am."

"Well, then, I guess you'll be playing teacher tonight." He winked at me. "Maybe you can teach me a few things with all your smarts."

"Well, if you want to lay me down, you'll have to obey me and listen." I giggled and he smiled at me with wide eyes.

"I'll lay you down right now if you want."

"Oh, Aiden. You wish," I said and then put a finger on his lips as George Ezra, the opening act, came on to the stage and the crowds of people started screaming and clapping.

FIFTEEN

Teddy bear heart

"LAST NIGHT WAS FANTASTIC," I said to Aiden as we walked to go and get breakfast. "This is the best birthday weekend ever."

"Ever ever?"

"Ever ever." I nodded and smiled joyously. "Sam Smith was amazing live. Even more amazing than I would have believed. I can't believe you got tickets and flew us here. That must have been so expensive."

"It's not the most expensive gift you'll ever get from me, I'm sure," he said and my heart almost stopped. I have to admit that once again I wanted to squeal and to call Liv. Was it just me or did that sound like he had plans to propose? I mean, obviously he's not going to be proposing this weekend (though if he did I wouldn't say no), but it seemed like maybe one day he would be.

"Oh?" I said softly, trying to pretend that my heart wasn't doing cartwheels.

"Let's go to the Ferry Building." He changed the subject, but his eyes were dancing. "I heard that they have this coffee called Blue Bottle that is amazing, and they have these cheese sandwiches at this place called Acme Bakery, and I know you love French bread."

"Let's do it!" I said excitedly.

"And if you're a good girl, I'll get you a cupcake from Miette's."

"What's Miette's?"

"This cute cupcake place right next to Blue Bottle."

"Oh, I'm so excited!" I practically skipped as we continued walking. "One thing, though?"

"Yes?"

"Can we catch a cab back?" I looked around at the hill we'd just climbed down. "I don't really fancy walking back up all these hills."

"Ha ha, that's fine. I have other ways for you to get exercise tonight."

"Oh yeah?"

"Oh yeah!" He licked his lips, and we both laughed. We continued walking in comfortable silence and I looked around me with interest. This was my first time in San Francisco and it was truly a beautiful city. It reminded me a bit of New York City, except for the fact that it was full of hills.

"Oh, look, a farmers market!" I said and ran over to a guy selling some paintings. "These are amazing."

"Thank you," the man said, and I watched as he painted something on the canvas in front of him.

"He's so good," I whispered to Aiden, and he nodded and looked around.

"Do you want a painting?" he asked me and I shook my head.

"No, no." I grabbed his hand. I didn't want him thinking that I was just using him to buy me lots of cool and expensive gifts. We continued walking through the different stalls until we came to a lady sewing what appeared to be teddy bears. I walked over to the table and stared at the handmade bunnies, owls and bears and my heart melted. They were all so cute and original.

"These are great." I smiled at the lady.

"Thanks, I make them all be hand myself." She smiled at me. "I use old sweaters and felt them."

"Oh, cool." I looked at them again and sighed. I knew I was too old to buy a teddy bear for myself, but I really wanted one.

"Looking for a gift?" she asked me, and I shook my head.

"No, I'm looking for myself." I laughed and she grinned at me.

"Hey, what do we have here?" Aiden joined me and smiled at the lady. "Hello."

"Hi." She smiled and then looked at me. "Is this your husband?"

"Oh no." I blushed. "He's my ..." My voice trailed off as I looked at Aiden. I felt slightly embarrassed to call him my boyfriend in front of him.

"I'm her boyfriend." He grabbed my hand and squeezed it. "And she's my insufferable girlfriend."

"You got that right," I joked and started to move away. "We should go."

"No, not yet." He shook his head. "I want to buy you one."

"Oh no, Aiden," I protested. "You don't have to do that."

"I want to." He smiled at me and picked up a small red bear with a yellow face and big black nose. There was a plaid green heart covering the stomach of the bear with red stitching around it and it looked absolutely adorable. "I want to get you this one." He handed it to me and then turned to the lady. "How much?"

"Twenty-eight dollars, please," she said eagerly, and I smiled at her as I held the bear to me. Aiden paid and then we left the stall.

"Thank you," I said quietly. "You didn't have to buy me anything."

"I wanted to," he said softly and pulled me to the side. "That bear represents me, and that heart covering the front of its body represents my heart and the love I have for you."

"Love?" I said, my eyes widening.

"Yes, love." He nodded and his eyes burned into mine. "It's always been you, Alice. I love you. And I want you to know that. My heart beats for you."

"I love you too," I said back. "Though my heart beats to keep my body running."

"Oh, Alice." He laughed and kissed me. "You do know that I didn't bring you here because Liv couldn't make your birthday, right? Liv couldn't make your birthday because I told her she needed to go out of town because I wanted to bring you to this concert and spend the weekend with you."

"Oh, Aiden, I had no clue. This is so romantic. Thank you."

"It's the least I could do." He laughed. "I mean, you took me to a BDSM store just for fun. I needed to make sure your birthday was a blast."

"Well, you have definitely done that." I kissed him on the cheek. "It's been perfect."

"Well, the best is yet to come." He grinned. "I have an amazing cake for you as well."

"Oh?"

"Yes!" He grabbed my hand. "You can eat it when we get back to the hotel."

"OH, WHAT A PERFECT DAY," I said as we walked back into our hotel room and I held my bear to my heart.

"It's not done yet." He smiled.

"Oh?"

"You still have your birthday cake and another surprise."

"What surprise?" I asked excitedly.

"Go into the bathroom and come out in ten minutes." He grinned. "Then you'll see."

"Ooh, okay." I squealed and put my stuff down. "Ten minutes?"

"Yes, come out in ten minutes. And no peeking."

"I won't peek." I laughed and hurried into the bathroom and waited. I wondered what my surprise was going to be. I was so excited I could barely stand it. I looked at my watch and groaned. Only one minute had passed. "Can I come out yet?" I shouted, but got no response. This was going to be the longest ten minutes in the history of time. I stared at my watch for what seemed like forever and then I opened the bathroom door slowly. "I'm coming out," I said as I walked out. "Aiden?" I said as my eyes adjusted to the dark.

"Oops, hold on," he said. "I forgot to light the candle." He nodded towards the night table. "The lighter is up there. Can you light it for me, please?"

"Okay." I stood there and walked over so that I could light the candle. "Oh." I giggled as a warm light filled the room." "Oh, Aiden," I said as I walked over to the bed. Aiden was lying on his back, naked. There were strawberries on his chest, covered in whipped cream and chocolate. I looked down his body and gasped as I saw whipped cream covering his penis. "Aiden, what's going on?" I laughed.

"Happy birthday," he sang out. "It's time for your birthday cake."

"You're my birthday cake?" I laughed.

"I'm good enough to eat." He grinned up at me. "And it's all yours."

"Aren't you hungry as well?" I said as I bent down and licked some whipped cream off of his chest. "This is yummy." I licked some more cream off and then licked my lips. "Let me take my clothes off first, so that they don't get dirty."

"Sounds good to me," he said huskily. "And yes, I'm hungry as well," he said as he stared up at me. "I hope that I'll get to eat after you."

"That can be arranged," I said as I pulled my clothes off.

"I have some more whipped cream."

"Hmm, maybe you should eat first, then?" I laughed.

"Do you want me to eat first?" He started to sit up eagerly and I pushed him back down.

"I'll eat first, thank you." I kissed him and then joined him on the bed. My naked body pressed against his, and I could feel the mixture of cream and sauces against my skin. "This feels weird." I laughed as I licked down his neck. I then moved to his nipples and sucked them gently and flicked them with my tongue before moving farther down. I then consumed his cock as if it were a banana split and it was the most delicious banana I'd ever eaten. Aiden groaned underneath me as I sucked on his cock, and I grinned to myself when he flipped me onto my back and spread my legs and started going down on me.

"Oh, Aiden!" I moaned as his tongue flicked against my clit and then entered me. "Oh, Aiden!" I screamed, unable to stop myself as waves of pleasure filled me.

"You taste better than cake," Aiden said as he kissed me after I'd climaxed on his face.

"And you have a tongue that's out of this world." I held him close to me. "Maybe you should be crowned the new Mr. Tongue."

"I think I'd like a new name."

"What about Mr. Big?"

"I like that." He grinned.

"No, there's a Mr. Big in *Sex in the City*. What about Mr. Cocky?"

"Make it Mr. Big Cocky and you've got a deal."

"What about Mr. Big Dick?" I said and squealed as he bit down on my lower lip.

"What about Mr. Pleasure Maker?" he said as he licked my lips.

"What about Mr. Pleasure?" I said finally and he nodded.

"I like that."

"Good. You're my Mr. Pleasure from now on."

"I'm your Mr. Pleasure, and I go all night long," he said and rolled me onto my back. "Are you ready for round one?"

"Yes, please." I nodded and cried out as he entered me swiftly with one deep thrust. This was definitely the best birthday ever.

SIXTEEN

The beginning of wonderful

"ARE YOU HOME?" LIV CAME running into my room as soon as she arrived back at the apartment.

"Yes." I sat up and jumped off of the bed so I could give her a hug. "We got back about an hour ago."

"Oh, Aiden's not here, is he?" She looked around with a disappointed face.

"No, Mr. Pleasure is not here." I laughed as her eyes widened.

"'Mr. Pleasure'?" She groaned. "Please no."

"That's his new name because—"

"No, no, no." She cut me off. "That is TMI, Alice."

"What?" I smiled widely. "I didn't even say why yet."

"I don't want to know about the magical things he does with his penis."

"Very magical things indeed." I laughed and grabbed her hands. "Let's go into the kitchen and have some hot chocolate and I'm going to tell you everything that happened this weekend, aside from how many times I—"

"Nope." Liv covered her ears. "I don't want to hear about how many times you orgasmed."

"I was going to say how many times we told each other 'I love you.'"

"You what?" she screamed and grabbed me. "This is the information you lead off with, Alice." She jumped up and down and squealed. "I can't believe you guys said 'I love you' already!"

"And he gave me a bear." I closed my eyes and relived the memories. "It was awesome."

"I still can't believe that my brother, Mr. Stick-up-his-ass, told you he loved you."

"He said that he's had a thing for me for a while." I grinned. "Just like me. He said he didn't want to rush anything or pressure me into getting into a relationship because he wanted to be sure that this wasn't just a crush for me. He wanted to know that it was an adult Alice making the decision and not an immature Alice."

"He did not say that." She rolled her eyes.

"I know. I couldn't believe it when he said that either." I laughed. "I wanted to say, what do you mean 'an immature Alice?' but I kept my mouth shut." I grinned at her. "I didn't want to ruin the bath."

"The bath? Don't you mean the moment?"

"The moment happened in a bath after we'd had birthday cake."

"Oh, that's so sweet. He got you a cake?"

"Kinda." I licked my lips.

"What do you mean kinda?"

"Well, he got me the toppings: whipped cream, strawberries, chocolate sauce and then put it on the base."

"What base?" Liv said and then made a face. "Oh my God, he was the base, wasn't he?"

"Yes, he was." I nodded and opened the fridge. "Best birthday cake I've ever had."

"Oh, Alice." She giggled. "I cannot believe my brother had the audacity to make himself the birthday cake."

"You can't?" I asked her with a questioningly look.

"Okay, I really can believe he had the audacity to do that." She opened the cupboard. "Want some cookies?"

"Do we have shortbread?"

"All the way from Scotland, baby." She nodded as she pulled out the box of Walkers Shortbread cookies.

"Yay!" I took out two cups from the cupboard and heaped the hot chocolate powder into them. "I've never been so excited, Liv. I guess I know what you feel like when you're with Xander."

"It's amazing, isn't it?" She smiled as she thought of her handsome fiancé. "Sometimes I just can't believe how lucky I am."

"I know," I said as I waited for the water to boil. "You know when you and Xander got engaged, I was a little jealous for myself. I felt so bad about it, but I was thinking to myself, will I ever have that? Will I ever have someone love me back so much that they would want to marry me?"

"Oh, Alice." Liv made a sad face. "I'm sorry you felt that way."

"Don't you dare feel sorry for me." I took the milk out of the fridge and turned to her. "It was selfish of me to even let myself think that in your moment. But I did, and it worried me. All I could think was that I didn't even know what I was going to do if it ended up that Aiden didn't really like me. I know I've dated other guys, but he's always been the one in my heart."

"Alice, you know how special you are. If it wasn't Aiden, it would have been some other fantastic guy."

"Some other fantastic guy wouldn't have been Aiden."

"And any other girl he would have ended up with wouldn't have been you."

"How did I get so lucky to have you as a best friend?" I asked Liv as I stirred the milk into the hot chocolate mix.

"I think it was fate," she said seriously. "I think we were meant to be best friends so that you could meet my brother and then we could end up as sisters."

"That's if Aiden and I get married."

"Oh, you'll get married." She laughed. "I'm positive of it, sis."

"Oh God, that means I gain Gabby as a sister, too."

"Don't take the Lord's name in vain, Alice." She laughed and picked up a cup. "Let's go through to the living room and watch some TV while we chat."

"That sounds good to me." I followed behind her and we both settled into the couch and made ourselves comfortable. "I'm going to miss you when you move out."

"I'm going to miss you, too." We stared at each other for a few seconds, and we both looked at each other in surprise when the doorbell rang.

"Who's that?" I asked, my heart skipping a beat, hoping it was Aiden.

"No idea." She shrugged. "I thought Xander was going home." We both jumped up and hurried to the door as the doorbell rang again. "It has to be Aiden." She rolled her eyes. "He's the only one I know who's so impatient that he has to ring the doorbell multiple times in seconds."

"Oh Liv," I said, but I hurried to the door and opened it. "Oh, it's Aiden and Xander." I grinned at Aiden, who looked me over with an expression of desire on his handsome face.

"Hello to you, too." Aiden swooped in and picked me up and gave me a big kiss.

"What are you guys doing here?" Liv stepped forward and gave Xander a kiss on the cheek.

"We didn't want to leave our two favorite girls home alone." Aiden grinned as he put me back down. "Plus, I didn't want you to get into any trouble."

"What trouble are we going to get into on a Sunday night, Aiden?"

"Knowing you two, I'd say a lot of different things," Xander said with a laugh as Liv hit him in the shoulder.

"We were just about to watch TV, actually." I kissed Aiden lightly on the lips. "And we were just drinking hot chocolate."

"I love chocolate," he said and sucked on my lower lip.

"We know," Liv said loudly and cleared her throat.

"You told her already?" He groaned as he looked at his sister. "Alice!"

"What? She's my best friend."

"And I'm her brother." He shook his head.

"I'll have to tell Mom and Dad that they deserve an award," Liv said with a small smile.

"Award for what?" Aiden asked her with a curious expression.

"An award for creating Mr. Pleasure," she teased, and I watched as Aiden's face went red.

"I'm going to kill you, Alice." His fingers came up under my arms and started to tickle me. "I'm seriously going to kill you."

"No." I tried to push him off as I started squirming and laughing. "You can't tickle me. No!" I shrieked as his hands kept up their assault. "Aiden, please!" I caught his hand and tried to stop him. "I won't tell her anything else."

"Liar." He pinched my nose. "If you don't stop lying, it's just going to keep growing."

"I'm not lying." I giggled. "I mean, obviously I'm going to tell her stuff—"

"I'm right here, guys," Liv interjected. "I can still hear you."

"Maybe we should give them some privacy," Xander said and grabbed her around the waist. "Maybe we can go to your room."

"Nope," Liv said and shook her head. "Alice and I were planning on watching TV and talking. If you guys want to stay, you can just watch TV with us."

"Do we have to?" Aiden made a face and looked at me. "I had much more exciting plans for us."

"They will have to wait," I said and grinned at Liv. "We had a girls' night planned. If you guys want to stay, you'll just have to participate."

"What does that mean?" Xander asked.

"It means I'm painting your nails." Liv grabbed his hands. "You can choose the color."

"Ugh." Xander groaned, but he was still smiling. "I'm going to need a beer—or ten."

"Coming right up," I said and pulled away from Aiden. "Do you want anything?"

"Besides you in the bed right now?" he said softly as he whispered in my ear.

"Aiden," I groaned as he caressed my back. "Do you want anything to drink?"

"Besides your juices as you come in my mouth?" he whispered again, and my face grew bright red.

"Aiden!" I slapped his shoulder. "Go into the living room with Xander now."

"Yes, Aiden." Liv pointed her finger at her brother. "You'd better behave."

"Or what?" he retorted back.

"Or I'm going to show you what happens to boys who don't behave." I grabbed the top of his shirt and pulled him towards me. "I bought a paddle online and it arrived while we were gone."

"A paddle, huh?" His eyes sparkled down at me.

"Yes, a paddle." I pulled him even closer to me. "And I'm not afraid to use it."

"I hope you're not afraid to feel it as well," he said softly. "'Cause my hand is itching to give you a good spanking right now."

"Oh yeah?" I said and then whispered against his lips, "I think I'll have to make sure that doesn't happen, then. I think tonight I'll handcuff you to the bed."

"Oh yeah?" he said and tugged on my lower lip.

"I'm going to tease you until you beg me to take you." I licked his lower lip and he groaned.

"What if I beg you right now?" he said and pulled me into him so that I could feel his hardness against my stomach. "What if I begged you to take me right now?"

"It wouldn't matter." I gave him a quick kiss and pulled away from him. "I'm the one in charge right now. We'll go to bed when I say." I watched his jaw drop open in surprise, and I grinned as I walked back down the corridor to the living room while swaying my hips. I looked behind me as I got to the living room door and I saw Aiden just standing there, looking at me with narrowed eyes and a huge grin on his face. I walked into the living room feeling warm and excited. This truly was the beginning of something wonderful and adventurous between us.

SEVEN TEEN

Waiting is part of the fun

"NO MONOPOLY TONIGHT," LIV SAID as we all sat around her parents' dining room table. She spoke directly to Aiden and he made a face at her.

"Fine," he said as he held my hand under the table. "What do you want to play, then?"

"I don't care," she said and then looked at Elizabeth. "What do you want to play?"

"Who, me?" Elizabeth blushed. "I'm just happy to be here. I'm surprised I was invited." She looked at me. "I wasn't sure how you'd feel about me being here."

"Oh, I'm fine." I laughed. "You were a great actress, but you were always nice. I'm glad you're here. Liv and I need another girl in the group."

"Aww, thanks. I'm so happy to be here." She smiled at me and then at Liv. "I'm so glad to make some new friends in town."

"Oh, I thought you made friends quite easily," Scott said with a weird look on his face.

"I'm glad I gave you that impression," she responded with a tight look on her face.

"I think we all got that impression, didn't we?" Scott looked around the table, and I could see that he looked slightly annoyed. Liv and I gave each other a look and I was dying to talk to her about the weirdness between them. What was going on there?

"I'd be happy to show you around town," Henry said from his seat next to Scott. His green eyes looked friendly as he smiled at her and he was clearly oblivious to the tension in the room. Typical man!

"Oh, thanks." She smiled back. "I'd like that."

"I'm sure you would," Scott said and then chugged his beer down. "So what are we going play, then?"

"I think we should play whatever Liv and Xander want to play," I said. "This is their game night."

"Yeah. I agree," Chett said and jumped up. "Sorry, guys, but I just realized that there's a NASCAR race on. I'm going to check it out. I think Mom and Dad have gone to bed, so I can change the channel."

"Chett!" Liv said and laughed. "Fine, go and watch your car racing."

"Hey, at least I came." He grinned. "Gabby didn't even show up."

"That's not a shock." Liv laughed and Xander wiped his forehead.

"I can't say I'm complaining." He made a face. "I've had enough awkward with Gabby to last the rest of my life."

"I know!" Liv clapped her hands. "Let's play truth or dare."

"Okay." Aiden nodded and sat back. "Is everyone in?"

"Yes," Liv, Xander, Scott, Henry, Elizabeth and I all said in chorus.

"Okay," Liv said. "Let's go in a circle. I'll start the questions and Elizabeth will be first up, then we'll just go round, okay?"

"Okay." We all nodded.

"Okay, truth or dare?" she asked Elizabeth.

"Truth," she said with a smile and made a face. "I hope I don't regret this."

"Why did you take the fake-girlfriend job?" Liv asked and I was surprised by her question, though I had wondered myself.

"Because I needed the money." Elizabeth looked at me. "I'd lost my job, and this was the first offer I'd got and I needed to pay rent. Plus, Aiden didn't seem sleazy, and when he explained to me that he was trying to see if the girl he loved really cared about him or was just playing games, I kinda felt for him. And then I met Alice, and I knew that they were perfect for each other." She smiled at me. "I have to admit I felt bad, especially when I had those cuff marks on my wrists. I thought it was going too far, but I think Aiden got a bit carried away."

"I did." He nodded and kissed me on the cheek. "I wanted to see how far I could push you. I'm sorry. I just wanted to see what you'd do. I kinda liked seeing you jealous."

"Aiden!" I hit him in the shoulder. "You're awful."

"I know. I'm sorry."

"Guys." Liv grinned at us. "This is Elizabeth's time. You guys will have your chance later."

"Sorry." I grinned back at her.

"So do you have a job now?" Liv asked Elizabeth and she shook her head.

"Not yet." She sighed. "I'm still looking."

"Maybe I can help," Scott interjected. "I'm looking for some help."

"Oh, really?" Elizabeth looked at him, her expression unsure.

"Yeah, we'll talk later." He nodded.

"Okay," she said, and Liv looked at me with a huge grin. The game continued on for a few rounds and almost all of us chose dares instead of truth. It was crazy when Xander dared Henry to kiss Elizabeth. I wasn't sure what he was playing at, but if looks could kill, Scott would have killed both Xander and Henry.

"Okay, you're up, Aiden," Liv said. "Truth or dare."

"Truth," he said simply, and Liv looked thoughtful for a while before speaking.

"When did you realize you had a thing for Alice?" she asked softly, and my heart thudded as I stared at him. This was something I'd been wondering as well and I loved her for knowing to ask him.

"Aww." He grinned and looked at me. "I should have known this was coming."

"Answer, please." I grinned back at him.

"I first knew I was falling for Alice many summers ago," he said and held my hands to his heart. "It was the summer after I'd graduated from college. I was in the kitchen with Mom, and you came sailing through the doors like sunshine and rainbows and you gave me a huge smile and my breath was just taken away. I remember standing there and staring at you and thinking that you'd blossomed into a beautiful, beautiful girl."

"Wow," I said as I gazed into his blue eyes. I could remember that exact moment and it struck me that the emotions and feelings I'd been feeling that summer weren't just a part of my imagination, but very real.

"That was when I knew that Alice was the one." He chuckled and looked embarrassed. "That sounds corny, doesn't it?"

"No." I shook my head and then I thought about something. "So you knew before I crept into your bed?"

"Crept into his bed?" Henry looked amused. "What?"

"Not now, Henry," Xander said and shook his head at his brother.

"Yes," Aiden said with a smile. "I knew I was falling for you before that night."

"I didn't know." I stared at him in amazement. "I can't believe I didn't know that."

"Why do you think I went ahead with it when you slipped into my bed?" He laughed. "I don't just sleep with anyone."

"I'm glad to hear that." I laughed and snuggled into him. "I was so scared to fall for you. I was so scared that I was going to ruin everything. You're my best friend's brother, and I thought that I jeopardized everything that night, especially because you never spoke about it to me again."

"You were too young, Alice. I wanted you to date, go through college and see how you felt after you'd had a few more life experiences. I didn't want to start something with you and then have you regret it and change your mind. I don't know if I could have coped with that."

"I understand." I nodded and kissed him. "Thank you."

"Aww, who knew my big brother was such a softie?" Liv smiled happily. "Now we're one big family."

"Not quite." Xander laughed. "Don't go jumping the gun, Liv."

"I think it's fair to say not yet." Aiden squeezed my hand and then stroked my hair. "We'll all be one big official family one day."

"I'm going to be Mrs. Pleasure one day?" I asked happily.

"I think so." He laughed and kissed me softly. "As long as you pass all of the tests."

"Tests?" I pouted.

"You know." He grinned at me. "Our special tests."

"I'm ready to take an exam right now." I stroked his thigh and he groaned.

"I'm ready to test you," he replied, and Liv groaned.

"Enough, guys!" She held her hands up. "This game night is rated PG." She giggled. "You guys have to go somewhere else for the rated X nights."

"Oh, don't you worry about that, little sis," Aiden said and winked at me. "I've already got our first X-rated night out planned."

"You do?" I asked him, my heart racing. "Where?"

"You'll just have to wait and see." He grinned. "The waiting is part of the fun."

EPILOGUE

You know when you know

I'D ALWAYS WONDERED HOW I would know that I'd met the one. I'd always wondered what true love was. I can tell you now that once you have it, you'll stop wondering. Once you have true love, you'll know it from the bottom of your being. You'll know because there is nothing that will ever replace or top that feeling. Nothing will ever live up to the feeling of simply seeing your loved one's face. Once you have true love, you don't wonder if it's real. No, once you have true love, you just want to bottle it up so that you never lose or forget that feeling. Once you've found the one, you'll know what it really means to be complete.

"Do you know how happy I am, Alice? Do you know how much I love you?"

"Yes," I said as I lay next to him in the bed. "I know because I feel the same way."

"We're really lucky—you know that, right?"

"I know." And then I nibbled down on his chest and looked up at him. "I still can't believe you faked being a Dom."

"I'm surprised you forgave me so quickly." He pinched my ass. "Is it because I'm so lovable?"

"I forgave you so quickly because I know I've been a bit immature myself in the past. But pull a stunt like that again and you're going to really have to make it up to me big time."

"Oh?" He laughed. "I think I've made it up to you, don't you?"

"Why? Because you like to tie me up and spank me?"

"No, because I let you tie me up as well." He laughed. "And because I let you talk me into going to a couples massage."

"You went to the couples massage because you thought we'd have sex in the pool." I laughed.

"How was I to know that there would be five other couples in the same pool?" He groaned. "That was not sexy."

"It was fun, and we both felt more relaxed afterwards."

"True." He pulled me close to him and kissed the top of my head. "I always feel relaxed when I'm with you."

"Really?" I held him close to me.

"Yup. You make me relaxed and happy, Alice. You're my everything. You're the best thing that's ever happened to me."

"You're only saying that because I booked us a room at Kat's Corner again next week."

"Well, are you not excited to try out the sex swing?" His fingers grazed my lips as he stared at me.

"Well, about that …" I said and sat up. "I have a little surprise for you."

"You do?" His eyes widened in glee. "What is it?"

"It's an early birthday present." I jumped out of the bed and grabbed a big plastic bag that was next to my suitcase. "I figured maybe you might want it early."

"Ooh, what is it?" He grabbed the bag and pulled out the box holding the doorjamb sex sling that I'd bought him. "Wow," he said with a huge smile as he stared at the box. "This is hot. Seriously hot."

"We can try it now, if you want?" I winked at him and laughed as he jumped out of bed and ripped open the box. I stared at him while he set the sex sling up and smiled to myself. This was what it was to be in love. This is what it meant to be adventurous and fun loving. I didn't need to play games with Aiden. I didn't need to try and make him jealous. I knew I loved him and he loved me and that was enough. Between our adventures in and out of the bedroom, I had enough to deal with.

"You need to hold onto these straps and put your feet in here." Aiden pulled me over to him and lifted me up so that I could fit in the sex sling.

"I hope it doesn't fall down," I said as I glanced up at the top of the door with a worried expression.

"Don't worry," he said and gave me a quick kiss. "I'll be here to catch you if you fall. I'll always catch you, Alice. I'll always be here to catch you," he said and my heart melted as his eyes glittered into mine right before he entered me with one long, deep thrust.